getting
clean with
stevie green

ALSO BY SWAN HUNTLEY

We Could Be Beautiful
The Goddesses

getting clean with stevie green

SWAN HUNTLEY

GALLERY BOOKS

New York   London   Toronto   Sydney   New Delhi

G
Gallery Books
An Imprint of Simon & Schuster, Inc.
1230 Avenue of the Americas
New York, NY 10020

This book is a work of fiction. Any references to historical events, real people, or real places are used fictitiously. Other names, characters, places, and events are products of the author's imagination, and any resemblance to actual events or places or persons, living or dead, is entirely coincidental.

First Gallery Books trade paperback edition January 2022

GALLERY BOOKS and colophon are registered trademarks of Simon & Schuster, Inc.

For information about special discounts for bulk purchases, please contact Simon & Schuster Special Sales at 1-866-506-1949 or business@simonandschuster.com.

The Simon & Schuster Speakers Bureau can bring authors to your live event. For more information or to book an event, contact the Simon & Schuster Speakers Bureau at 1-866-248-3049 or visit our website at www.simonspeakers.com.

Interior design by Davina Mock-Maniscalco

Manufactured in the United States of America

10 9 8 7 6 5 4 3 2 1

Library of Congress Cataloging-in-Publication Data TK

ISBN 978-1-9821-5962-7
ISBN 978-1-9821-5963-4 (ebook)

Dedication T/K

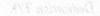

Visible mess helps distract us from the true source of the disorder.
MARIE KONDO

Trying to define yourself is like trying to bite your own teeth.
ALAN WATTS

PART I

yes

CHAPTER 1

stevie

It's so hard to know who you are.

That's why I'm constantly looking in the mirror.

Who am I?

Who am I now?

What about now?

I check myself out from various angles, trying to clock a change. That's what people do in moments of transition, right?

If nothing else, I find the sight of my reflection soothing. In my head, I'm a mess, but in the mirror, I'm solid. I'm a woman who has her life in order. I dress well, I do my hair, I have an open, friendly face. You would ask me for directions. You would trust me with your children.

If I were a town, I would probably be my hometown. La Jolla, California, is a place with a winning exterior. It dresses well. It's ordered. It's warm. Its lucky placement on a breathtaking portion of the Southern California coastline means it's never had to try too hard. An image of La Jolla is an image of an easy life.

Considering the fortunate circumstances under which I grew up, there should have been no reason for my life to turn into a trash fire.

Except for that it did.

Why?

Because of one incident. I would call this one the inciting indent.

Unfortunately, the inciting incident had been on my mind all the time since moving home six months earlier, but it also wasn't the point.

"The point," I said to myself in the rearview, "is about starting over now."

The light turned green. It was another perfect, sunny day in La Jolla, and I was driving to the house of a new client, Lauren Strong. I liked to use my car time to practice my spiel, and this is what I did now.

First, I quelled any potential embarrassment with my usual reminder: *If anyone sees me talking to myself, they'll assume that I am on the phone.*

I cleared my throat.

And then I began.

"Do you have a picture in your mind of the person you want to become? And a profound sense of how you'll *feel* when you become that person? Are you *almost* there, but not quite yet? If so, then let me help you!

"The difference between a *clean life* and a *clean enough life* might look small from afar, but it's actually the Grand Canyon. Yes, you can put on a show for people. Yes, you can lie. Yes, you can live in a palace and wear great clothes and say the right things, but if your closets are packed to the brim with stuff you don't need, and if you also feel a little bit dead inside, then who cares how sparkly your life looks to other people? If it doesn't *feel* clean to *you*, then it's not."

I was practicing my spiel for Lauren, of course, but I was also practicing for a more successful future, possibly one that included a TV spot or a book tour—some professional event that starred me, a woman who was mic'd and teeming with unbreakable confidence. There would be a newly waxed stage and a rapt audience and somewhere nearby, a poster that said, STEVIE GREEN, DECLUTTERING GURU.

"Now you're probably like, 'Well, okay, I think my life could be cleaner, and why isn't it already?'"

I paused here for dramatic effect.

"Because you don't know what you want. And that's okay. Not knowing what you want makes you like everyone else. It also really sucks, and you don't need to live that way anymore.

"The solution is simple, but there are no shortcuts. Actually, we're taking the long way to make sure we haven't left anything out. In order to figure out what you really want, we're going to start by getting rid of everything you *don't* want. You know that guess-and-check thing you used to do in math class? Have you heard the song 'The Long Way Around'? It's like that. By saying goodbye to all the incorrect answers, we'll land at the right one, and the right one is your clean and honest life."

Out of habit, I opened the center console and counted the bottles of screw-top chardonnay with my hand. One, two, three. I didn't want to drink them. That's why I kept them close by: to remind myself. I'd imagine the taste of buttery wine and feel the hot prick at the back of my throat and think, *No thanks*. They were like a stress ball. They reduced my stress. Plus, they were tiny and taking up barely any room in my life, so who cared.

"Your stuff is holding you back and weighing you down! You're drowning in it," I said, slamming the center console shut. "But not anymore. It's time to free yourself. It's time to become who you are."

CHAPTER 2

stevie

Lauren Strong was a stay-at-home mom whose shopping problems had led her to the brink of divorce. That's how she'd put it in her message to me.

My husband's nickname for me is Overkill.

We're on the brink of divorce.

The brink part might have had extra meaning for Lauren since she lived at the edge of a cliff. Her house was a modern marvel, four stories high, with an industrial, unfinished vibe. Basically it looked like some rectangles in a pile, set just slightly askew. Cement, wood, glass. The elements in their naked forms were easy to identify.

I turned off the engine and reminded myself that I wasn't a see-through person.

If you believe in you, then she'll believe in you.

Then I got out of the car, a brand-new Volvo station wagon that made me look like a higher earner than I was, and walked with gusto toward the wooden gate just in case anybody was watching. I often did things like this—with the understanding that somebody might be watching. It was good, because it made me try harder to be the person I wanted to be all the time. If my ex-friend/life destroyer Chris saw me right now, she'd see what I saw in the mirror: a woman who was solid, and on her way somewhere.

In the six months since moving home, I hadn't seen Chris, not even once, but I was always expecting to see her. She'd been a central character in my head ever since we'd stopped talking.

From the sidewalk, Lauren's architectural choices gave the impression that she was a minimalist, but she'd warned me about this in her message.

It's not real!

When I opened the gate, I saw what she meant. Lauren's suspiciously green lawn, which I'd realize in a second was Astroturf, was almost invisible underneath an ocean of Fisher-Price goods. The plastic primary colors shone with manufactured radiance under the sun-filled sky. It either looked like the wildest dreams of a child who watched a lot of commercials or a genetics lab for toys, because everything was multiplied. Those red cars with the yellow tops that every kid has? I quickly counted six of them.

And then I imagined lining them all up and putting the other repeat items together, because that was always the first step: ordering the mess so you could see it clearly, just as you would with a jigsaw puzzle. You'd put the like colors in a pile. Obvious. Well, it was obvious to me, but apparently it was not so obvious to other people, who were stuck in amateur hour gathering up the edges first: a total mistake, because then you had to hop all the other pieces over the edge later. Why do that? The acrobatics were unnecessary.

I quickly assessed that 75 percent of Lauren's Fisher-Price goods needed to go, and further assessed that with caffeine in my system and my Hokas on my feet, I could get the job done myself within forty-five minutes. I felt a little bit high thinking about this, because that's how much I enjoyed the act of making sense of a life, or at least of an area. I loved organizing for the same reason that I loved vacuuming: immediate, tangible results, which were so unlike the slow, mysterious shifts of the internal self.

Inconveniently, I wasn't going to be able to get the job done by myself, however, because the decluttering business doesn't work that way. People want to hash things out first. People want to be heard. Sometimes they want to have long conversations about what a particular hat or brooch or dented-ass picture frame means to them, and mostly they want to make excuses for why they need things they don't really need. I'm usually patient except for the times I want to wring a client's neck and scream, *Make a choice, sister!*

It was for this reason that I'd recently decided to implement a five-second rule. Lauren would be the first client to hear about it.

"You're here!" Lauren called from the doorway with so much enthusiasm that I could tell she was lonely. It made me feel better. Lauren, barefoot, with her morning hair all tangled up, was vulnerable. She had issues, and she wasn't trying to hide them. She was being her real, messy self.

"Hey, Lauren!"

I jogged up the steps like I meant it, because first impressions are everything.

———————

Like many of my clients, Lauren Strong was a person who probably ate cereal in bed at odd hours while thinking about doing things rather than actually doing them. The inside of her house, like the outside, seemed, at first glance, like the work of an expert minimalist. "But I'm a repeat offender," she said, flopping her head to the side in a posture of defeat. "I buy something once, and then I keep buying it."

Lauren had given me a pamplemousse LaCroix and invited me to sit on her modern couch, which had only half a backrest and was made of "recycled something-something, I forget what Todd said." Todd was Lauren's husband, a semi-well-known green architect who'd lived at an ashram when he was younger, so he didn't like *things*, Lauren explained with an eye roll. "So I hide them. It's bad. The yard is driving him insane. I can't get a divorce over a freaking *yard*. Even though, I know! The yard isn't the problem. *I'm* the problem. I just want Finny to have everything I never had. And I want to have everything I never had, too. I haven't shown you *my* toys yet."

Lauren, who weighed four pounds and moved around with the frantic energy of a small bird, sprang off the couch and grabbed my wrist and pulled me down the bare hallway while explaining that Finny, her one and only son, age five, had "a million friends who come over to play." That was her defense for all his toys.

We arrived at a closed door. Lauren stopped, and sighed loudly, and put her hand on my waist, which was uncomfortable, but not surprising. Most people, it turns out, think it's fine to touch you after they've hired you.

She winced, then said, "While I was potty training Finny, I'd give him a stuffed animal every time he dropped a deuce. That's when Todd started calling me Overkill."

She scooted her knotty bun to the side and looked up at me like she needed encouragement, so I gave her some.

"After this," I said, "Todd's not going to call you that anymore, don't worry."

She didn't seem convinced. "I think Todd's over me in general."

I didn't know what to say to that, so I just smiled in a way that said, *I understand.*

"When I open this door," Lauren said, "you're going to be disappointed."

"I'm sure I've seen worse," I said, wondering if it would be true.

"I grew up poor and now I'm making up for it. Did you grow up poor?"

I avoided the question because I knew my answer was not very relatable. "I've had many clients who want to give their kids everything they never had. It makes sense. And it's all okay."

"It's all okay," Lauren echoed, perking up. "I like you."

Then she pushed the door open, revealing what must have been at least fifteen Vespa scooters in different colors.

"Eighteen," she said.

"They're beautiful," I said. They were also very clean, and gleamed prettily under the fluorescent ceiling lights. "When was the last time you rode one?"

"It's been a while." Lauren bit her finger. "You're going to make me get rid of all of them, aren't you?"

"I'm not going to *make* you do anything," I assured her. "Let's go through the rest of the house. Then we'll sit down and schedule your Freedom Day."

"Freedom Day?" Lauren asked, her eyes like a kid. "I like the sound of that."

"Everybody does. Because that's all anybody wants, right? To feel free."

———

I was sure the rest of Lauren's house couldn't possibly be as bad as the garage and the yard because it looked so tidy, but I was wrong. Lauren's makeup collection took up six large drawers. She owned forty-one pairs of sneakers and seventeen tennis rackets even though she'd stopped playing tennis at age twenty-five, when a buff senior citizen—"bodybuilder buff, and I'm serious"—had smacked her in the face with a racket by accident.

Lauren tipped her head back. "See the hatch marks on my nose?"

"No," I said, "but I believe you."

The walk-in closet in the master bedroom was stuffed full of clothes, and 90 percent of them were Lauren's. Todd owned almost nothing, and what he did own he had multiples of: jeans, white shirts, blazers, loafers. I respected a person in uniform because I'd recently become one myself, although I wasn't quite as strict as Todd. I had multiple styles of tops and bottoms. From afar, they probably all looked the same, but they were not. Lauren, on the way up the stairs, had identified my personal style as "athleisure meets business," which I thought was great and planned to say to somebody else later if it came up.

By the time we got to Finny's room on the upper level, I wasn't surprised to find a stuffed animal zoo. "One animal for each letter of the alphabet," Lauren said. "Ish."

There must have been at least three hundred animals piled in a furry mess along the wall, so Lauren's math was definitely off, but I didn't tell her that. I told her that it was all fine and okay and that the important thing was that she'd reached out to me, and that's when, on the way back down the floating stairs made of light blond wood and mysteriously held together by only two thin black metal columns, she revealed that it hadn't exactly been her idea. "It was my lover's idea. He doesn't want me to get divorced because he says it will ruin our arrangement."

Back on the couch, Lauren divulged more about their arrangement, which consisted of long beach walks while Todd was at work and also beach sex. "You know all the crevices between the cliffs down at Blacks? We like those when the tide's low."

"A nice place to hide," I said.

"On a Mexican serape, usually," Lauren finished, leaning into the half-backed couch that couldn't really support her.

Then she told me more. Her lover's name was Vincent. He drove a Beamer and wore James Perse shirts and listened to Nickelback and his feet were super clean. Oh, and he worked for his dad's company, but, like, vaguely, because he didn't ever go to the office? The company sold—well, whatever, Lauren couldn't remember. But the point was that because Vincent was never at the office, he was always at a coffee shop with his laptop, and that's where they'd met. "We were standing in line together at the Living Room and he told me I smelled nice. And he's *hot*. And emotionally unavailable, which probably makes him hotter?"

Lauren knew it was a dead end, but she felt like her soul was at a dead end too, so it seemed to match.

"Sometimes I wonder if I want to get caught," she said. "Like I'm subconsciously trying to blow up my life, you know what I mean?"

"I do," I said.

"Or maybe I'm just bored." Lauren moaned, then covered her face with a small, firm pillow.

"I get it," I said. "Your life looks perfect, but it's not."

Lauren whipped the pillow away from her face. "Yes! That's it! My life looks so nice and it's so much pressure! I feel like I'm not allowed to complain. People all over the world are starving. Icebergs are melting. And my brothers are totally broke. I can't even talk to them. So what am I supposed to do? Get over it and book another facial? My face is falling off."

Lauren pulled down hard on her cheeks, revealing the gross red parts underneath her eyeballs. I told myself not to look away.

"Because that's what I've been doing. Facials and shopping. I used to make myself get dressed and go to the mall, like a real outing, but I don't even do that anymore. I just sit in here all day and click *Add to Cart, Add to Cart, Add to Cart.* The only time I pretend to be productive is when the cleaning lady comes. And obviously I work out because I can't be depressing *and* fat, oh my god."

"Lauren," I said calmly, "I hear you. And now I'm going to tell you what your real problem is. Are you ready?"

Lauren seemed shocked that I would speak to her with such authority, but I could tell she liked it, too. This is what people were paying me for: to tell them the truth. I delivered it in one clear sentence.

"You don't know what you want."

Lauren blinked hard, then shook her head out like she'd been smacked. "Whoa."

"Right now, your life is full of a lot of things that are weighing you down. We're going to get rid of those things. It's time to become yourself."

Lauren's eyes were wide open now. "It's like I was poor and then I got rich and I bought all this stuff, but it didn't work. I'm not happy, and when I look around I'm like, *Whose life is this? Who buys* eighteen *Vespa scooters?*"

It was a good question, and one that was beyond my pay grade, so I didn't answer it.

"Here's how the process works. For every item, we ask the same question."

I always paused here to make sure the client was paying attention.

"What is it?" Lauren asked.

I held out my right palm. "Yes." And then my left. "Or no."

Lauren pulled her chin back into her neck and gave me a side-eye. "That's it?"

"That's it. And you have five seconds to answer."

"*Five?* What if I need to try something on?"

I maintained my authoritative demeanor, knowing that it mattered more than what I was actually saying. If you present information with total confidence, people buy into it. That is the nature of people. "You don't," I said.

"You're intense," Lauren said.

"I'm productive."

Lauren planted her hand on my shoulder. "You're exactly who I need right now."

I felt a wave of relief, which I didn't let register on my face at all.

"Anything that's not a yes is a no. 'Maybe' means no. 'Later' means no. 'Sometimes,' 'sort of,' 'potentially'—no, no, no. When something truly belongs in your life, you know it in your gut immediately, no question."

Lauren told me she understood the concept and appreciated it, but she didn't like it very much either. "Because if I apply that advice to Vincent, then I should get rid of him. And I don't know if Todd's a hard yes either. So, if neither of them is a yes, where would that leave me? Alone?"

"For now, let's only focus on tangible, store-bought items. The answers will come, I promise."

"You have a soothing voice," Lauren said. "You'd be, like, a really good narrator for a documentary or something."

"Thank you," I said, and of course I thought of Sigourney Weaver narrating *Planet Earth*, which I'd watched like it was my job while very hungover, but Lauren didn't need to know that.

"Should Finny be here to go through his toys?" she asked.

"No. You're the mother. You're in charge."

"Right. *I'm* in charge."

"*You're* in charge."

"Honestly," Lauren said, "I thought you were going to be . . . different? Like, I thought we were going to do a ceremony and light a candle and chant and stuff."

"Waste of time."

Lauren gazed at the top of my head in a way that made me wonder if my hair was sticking up. "How long have you been organizing?"

"Forever," I told her. "I've always been very organized. And I started my business six months ago. I flew down from San Francisco to help my mom move and then I ended up staying."

"Wait, how old are you?"

"Thirty-seven."

"Me too!" Lauren bounced on the hard couch. "I'm a Scorpio."

"Great," I said.

"It means I'm diabolical, but really I'm not." Lauren fluttered a hand. "Anyway, I want to know everything about you now! Do you have a husband? A boyfriend? Kids? You look really fit. Are you a runner?"

I smiled. Then I checked my watch. "Yes, I run," I said warmly. "And no, I'm not dating anyone."

"I hate running," Lauren said. "But I love your hair." She reached out to touch it like it was hers. "Where do you get it done?"

"Oh, there's this place downtown," I said. "I just cut it off. It used to be really long."

"Wow," Lauren said. "You're brave. When did you cut it?"

"Six months ago."

Lauren squinted at me like somebody who felt she possessed a deep well of wisdom within her. "A lot happened for you six months ago."

Before I could agree, she asked me if I wanted a glass of wine. "I know it's not even noon yet, but you only live once, right?" She giggled self-consciously.

"Oh, I'm on a cleanse," I told her.

"Let me take a wild guess about when your cleanse started." Lauren tapped her cheek with her finger. "Six months ago."

I raised my eyebrows.

"Six months," Lauren said again, but emptily this time. Her demeanor had shifted from overly peppy to completely still. "Listen. I have to tell you something."

I thought she was going to fire me.

"I've been trying to stop drinking, but I can't. How have you gone six whole months?"

"I'm just taking a break," I said. "It's not a big deal."

"I can't even go *two days*," Lauren said, her face strangling itself in worry lines.

"You will," I promised her. "When you're ready, you'll just stop."

Lauren was unconvinced. "I hope so."

"Now listen," I said firmly. "After I leave, you're going to take a shower, put on an outfit you *like*, and go for a walk, okay? It doesn't matter how you *feel*. These are just the things you're going to *do*."

Lauren winced. "Do I have to?"

"Do you want to feel better?"

"Yes?"

"Don't *ask* yes. Say it like you mean it. Do you want to feel better?"

"Yes!" Lauren screamed. "Yes!"

At the door, she gave me a tight hug and I said, "I'm going to leave you with a question. Are you ready?"

"No."

"What would it feel like if you only had *one* of each thing? One scooter, one tennis racket, one man?"

"Oh god."

"I know."

"I hate that," Lauren said. "But I kind of love it, too."

"That's how everyone feels about change," I said. "You hate it until you love it."

We said our goodbyes, and I walked steadily across the Astroturf, aware that she was probably watching. In the car, my hand, out of habit, opened the center console and counted the bottles—one, two, three—and as I muttered my own wisdom to myself—*Change. You hate it until you love it*—I wondered if it was true.

CHAPTER 3

stevie

At the Pannikin, I ordered two green juices and a cappuccino because now that I wasn't drinking anymore, I deserved all the nonalcoholic beverages I wanted.

"That's a lot of liquid," the guy behind the register said, hitting the last grimy key on a pad that probably hadn't been switched out since my high school years.

I rolled my lips together and said nothing at first. Then I rotated the tip jar so the word TEEPS was facing out. "You spelled 'tips' wrong. Also," I said, stepping back to get a clearer view of the baked goods in disarray, "if you organized this display case better, I bet you'd sell more croissants."

"Um," the guy said, "I make minimum wage at this job, so."

"Right."

Feeling like a dick, I put a dollar in his misspelled tips jar, then took my beverages to a table behind a pillar so we wouldn't have to look at each other.

It's bold to sit at a café alone despite the fact that you are surrounded by young, hot couples and old, stable couples.

And if I didn't feel bold, then I could bury myself in my phone like everybody else. I'd also brought my iPad and two books in case I ran out of things to do, not that I would. I only had half an hour to kill before my next client visit with Stella Miller, a lawyer who lived down at Windansea.

I sucked my cappuccino down in three nonchalant gulps, then opened the Organizely app on my phone. As expected, my ranking hadn't changed since that morning. I was still number two, and the number one spot still belonged to Ursula de Santis, a petite seventy-year-old who looked like Mrs. Claus. Ursula had been decluttering since before "decluttering" was even a word, and somehow, she was still churning at a robotically productive rate.

Lucky for me, the Organizely app had only been invented a few months earlier, and this meant that Ursula was beatable and that I was going to beat her.

You need to know that I wanted to be La Jolla's number one decluttering guru very badly.

No, I *needed* to be number one very badly.

And if it didn't happen—well, there was just no world in which it wasn't going to happen.

I was going to fucking win.

Did I suspect that my intensity around this had something, if not everything, to do with the inciting incident? The incident that had taken me from the peak of Mount Everest to the bowels of the Mariana Trench? The incident that had lived underneath the surface of every thought I'd had and every word I'd spoken and every move I'd made for the last twenty years? The incident I wished that I could erase more than anything else?

Yes, I did.

Unfortunately, I was behind (4.6 with 42 reviews), and Ursula (4.8 with 69 reviews) showed no signs of slowing down.

I recognize that to the common onlooker, a gap of two-tenths of a point may not seem very wide.

But to me, it was the Grand Canyon.

I thumb-flicked the Organizely app away and moved on to Instagram. Midafternoon was when I did my daily post. My profile was simple.

Business name: Stevie Cleans.

Bio: Become who you are.

I had 608 followers so far, which I knew wasn't great, and which I was trying to address by listening to a business podcast about brand building hosted by an Australian woman named Henrietta, who had a forceful yet caramel-sweet voice. I'd never Googled Henrietta because I didn't want to smash my image of her as a wonderfully plump brunette with eyebrows that slanted up on the insides. People who have eyebrows like that are the nicest kinds of people.

Anyone in your life who isn't behind you 100 percent can sod off!

You are the master of your ship!

A social media presence is an absolute must!

I hated it when Henrietta talked about social media, because technology had never been my jam. Before Stevie Cleans, I didn't have social media. I used my laptop for Netflix and email, and sometimes I opened Word to make a list of the things I planned to change about myself.

Example:

Start meditating!!!
50 sit-ups/day
Read *New York Times* in morning
No more 3am burritos you are banned
Don't drink tonight
Pluck your eyebrows better dude

Anyway, the point I'm trying to make is that I'd never been that into machines. I was an analog person, one who enjoyed the tactile experience of trying out a new pen at the stationery store. It took me years too long to figure out how to burn a CD, and by the time I finally did, it was too late.

"Thank you, but a CD, Stevie? I don't even know what to do with this," my techie friend Phil said once.

I was equally resistant to texting when that fad hit. I'd call people instead, which now seemed like an invasion of privacy.

The texting example gave me hope. It proved that I was capable of evolving. Maybe I'd become just as accustomed to Instagram as I now was to texting. I still didn't like it, but thanks to Henrietta, I was getting out of my comfort zone, because that is where the growth lies!

I'd found a bunch of stock photos of tidy spaces online,

and I had them all queued up. I chose one—a close-up of some bath products in a suction-cup basket—and wrote a caption that I hoped would appeal to a wide audience.

Make more space with a snazzy shower basket!

I awarded myself three points for using the word "snazzy"—and then I heard my name.

"Stevie?"

And a wave of nausea curdled through me, because somewhere deep inside, I knew who it was before I actually saw her—her good jeans and her gray blazer and her very white shirt, so white that it might have been brand-new, and the coffee in her hand, and her hair, which was shorter now, a man's haircut, same as mine, and her mouth. It was a mouth I would have recognized as hers all these years later even if there hadn't been a face attached to it because it was so uniquely designed—the two peaks of her upper lip like pointy cartoon mountains and her broad lower lip like the side of a canoe, half-submerged in water.

"Stevie," Chris said again, her voice kind of hoarse. "Is that you?" She shifted her weight. "You cut your hair."

"I didn't know you came here," I said, trying to match her casual tone. My armpits prickled. I wondered if she was reading into my haircut, even though there was nothing to read into. I was a minimalist; I wanted less of everything, including hair, end of story.

"I work across the street." Chris motioned vaguely out the window. "Didn't your mom tell you?"

"I don't think so," I said, although right after the words had left my mouth I wondered if they were true. Mom had told me that Chris was a therapist now, but she hadn't told me where. Or at least I didn't think she had.

"Yeah, my name's on the sign," Chris said, and pointed at the wooden sign in front of the office building that looked like a gingerbread house. It was rich brown with stark white trim and surrounded by a neatly groomed hedge. "I'm a therapist now."

I sat up straighter, said the requisite "Good for you." And because I was so ready, because I'd envisioned this moment so many times, it was as if, in a way, it had already happened.

So then it did.

"Chris," I said, "I forgive you."

If these four little words came out sounding practiced, that was because they had been—for many years. After I said them, my cheeks burned brighter and froze colder at the same time, and the moment dripped with awkwardness so thick that I might have been seeing double.

Chris didn't blink for a long time, her big brown eyes doming out as far as they always had, and maybe slightly more. She was one of those people with eyes set at the precipice of their sockets, protruding like miniature balloons on the verge of escape. They were bulging one second and sensuous the next, and either way they gave the impression that Chris was both meditative and a risk-taker, a thoughtful being who lived comfortably on the edge.

The Pannikin was darkly lit, and especially shadowy in the corner I'd chosen, but the honey and amber rays that accentuated Chris's brown eyes glimmered anyway, as if to suggest that somewhere above the clouds, the sky was always blue. In other words, they seemed to suggest that she was enlightened in a way that I was not.

She stared straight at me, not blinking once, and said in a flat voice, "I would never have done that to you."

And I sank. I didn't move, but inside, I sank. Because I wanted her to say something different now, and after all this time, I thought she would.

"It's okay if you did," I said, trying to nudge her toward the answer I wanted. I even chuckled, as if to show her that I didn't really care that much. I wanted her to think that I'd let this whole thing go and that mentioning it now was just a formality, maybe one that spoke to my maturity. I was a fully formed adult person who tackled matters head-on rather than burying them under pleasantries.

Chris pushed her hands into the pockets of her good jeans, her eyes still on me. "I'm sorry for what happened to you. It was painful to watch."

Then she took her wallet out of her pocket, a plain black leather wallet with no identifiable logo, and pulled a card from it, a simple white card that was thicker and heavier than most business cards, and even though I didn't want to be impressed by this, I was.

"If you decide you'd like to get together at some point," she said, "give me a call. Your mom told me about your new business. Congratulations. I'd love to hear more about it."

She tilted her head and smiled, and then she was gone.

I wanted to watch her walk out the door and across the street, but of course I didn't watch her at all. Eyes back on my phone, thumb scrolling on autopilot, I imagined it instead:

Chris looking both ways before crossing, her coffee held a responsible distance from her body in case it spilled because she hadn't put a lid on the cup, and the easy way she walked past her name on that wooden sign, which was in the upper right-hand corner and written in blue.

CHAPTER 4

chris

I almost spilled my coffee, I was so nervous. Stevie looked
good, really good. I made it across the street, and the second I got into my office, I stationed myself by the window
and looked down at the Pannikin patio, hoping to catch another glimpse of her as I listened to the ring-ring-ring of the
phone. I was calling Kit.

"You didn't tell me Stevie cut her hair!"

"Doesn't it look nice?" Kit said. "A lot like yours, actually."

"She still thinks I'm responsible for those flyers, Kit."

There was a long pause.

"You know I didn't do it, right?" I said.

"Yes," Kit said. "I know you didn't do it."

Just then, Stevie walked across the patio. Like a gazelle, I
thought. That was how Stevie Green moved. Shoulders held
back, long legs gliding forward. She was graceful. She was
self-assured. And she was getting into the black Volvo wagon

parked right out front, which I should have known was hers. Kit had told me they'd bought matching cars.

Stevie turned on the engine. But for a moment, the car didn't move. She was probably punching an address into her phone. No, she was talking to someone. I could see her mouth moving. I wondered who it was.

"I still think Brad Rose did it," I said.

Kit had no response to that. I imagined her relaxed face, because her face was always relaxed, taking this in. Even though I liked Kit a lot, I found her annoyingly unreadable most of the time.

CHAPTER 5

stevie

Stella Miller's home was my dream home—an unassuming wooden structure with calm, clean lines that was right on the ocean, as in right on the ocean, as in the backyard was the sand. As I meandered up her curved walkway, which was flanked by pretty, wind-bent trees and benches made from large, flat stones, I was telling myself not to think about Chris.

Then I replayed everything again. What I'd said, what she'd said, what I should have said, what she didn't say. ("I'm sorry," and also, "You're right.") And then there was the future. What I planned to say the next time I saw her, if there was a next time. Maybe I'd make a next time. Maybe I'd call her. Or not.

I'd arrived at Stella's front door, where I took a breath and reminded myself that I was a professional decluttering guru who was very good at her job. Then, with a powerful fist—the fist of unbreakable confidence—I knocked twice.

When Stella opened the door, my first thought was, *I want to be you.*

She was tall and lanky and wearing a desert-brown blouse that draped glamorously over her angular body. Jeans with no holes. Salmon-colored leather loafers. Her face was classically configured and sort of stately, like the faces in Renaissance paintings, maybe, but with a freckled SoCal edge. Her eyes were aquamarine, almost too pretty to be real. And her voice, when she said my name, was deep and strong.

"Stevie Green?"

"Stella Miller, great to meet you." I shook her hand and tried to ignore the way my stomach flipped.

She invited me into her living room—brown leather furniture, a splashy geometric rug, mostly red, a bowl of seashells that said, *I belong right here on the beach*—and offered me a cup of rooibos tea in an indigo blue ceramic mug that I imagined she'd bought on a weekend trip to Taos or Mexico City or some other cool destination.

Then she sat next to me on the couch like she weighed nothing, which is not to say that she was too thin but rather to say that she seemed unaffected by the heaviness of her own thoughts, and explained that she really only needed help with (a) her clothes, and (b) her guest room, which was piled to the brim with documents, and by "to the brim" she meant that literally. "They're touching the ceiling in some areas," she said, laughing quietly.

What were the documents? Did she need them? They were old case files, and no, she didn't really need them. "I just like paper too much."

I wanted to tell her that I also liked paper too much, and I wanted to ask her where I could get that blouse in black, but I thought it would be best to maintain a professional distance. So I said, "Understood," in a friendly enough way and then began my spiel in my businesslike voice, which was slightly louder than my regular voice and which elongated my *R*s.

"It's rrreally simple. With every item, we ask the same question."

Stella raised her eyebrows. "What is it?"

I opened one palm. "Yes." Then the other. "Or no."

I held my breath, waiting for her response.

Stella chuckled. "That's the best thing I've ever heard."

"And you have five seconds to decide, because that's the speed at which your heart will know the answer. Anything that's not a yes is a no. Just trust yourself." I went on to explain the rest, ending with, "And that's why I call it Freedom Day."

"Genius." Stella looked at me with a new kind of attention then, trailing her eyes over my face, which made my cheeks flush. "You've put a lot of thought into this, haven't you?"

Before I could answer, my stomach made a noise. I coughed to cancel it out, but my cough was too late.

"Are you hungry?" she asked. "I have some cassava chips in the kitchen."

"No thanks," I said. "I'm fine."

Stella set her lovely mug onto her lovely table so gently that it didn't make a sound. "Shall I give you the tour then?"

I popped up like a cork shooting out of a bottle. "Yes!"

She showed me the guest room first, which, as she'd said, was so full of paper that it was touching the ceiling in some areas. "I even brought a stepladder in here so I could pile higher," she admitted. "I'm so bad." She'd carved a sort of hallway between the stacks that was narrower than her shoulders. "I shimmy in like this," she showed me, laughing at herself. I laughed this time, too, because it was hilarious: this gorgeously groomed woman inching sideways down the little road of her paper city.

Next we moved to her home office, which was tidy enough and sort of bohemian. Her desk was enormous and L-shaped, and on it were more stacks of paper, a rose-gold laptop, and a cloudy emerald-green lamp like the ones at old libraries. The view out the window was just water and air and a few birds, no land in sight. It was a view that said, *Anything is possible*.

I downsized my poetic thoughts as follows: "Nice view."

"Thanks."

Upstairs, Stella pointed to the closed door and said, "That's my partner's office, which we won't go into. And this is the bedroom." She stepped in, motioning for me to follow.

Her duvet was a dreamy lilac color—unexpected, and yet somehow better than expected. She opened the top drawer of her dresser. "Yeah, these clothes do need help," she was saying as I walked farther into the room.

On top of the dresser was a framed photo of Stella and another woman standing proudly in front of the house on the day they'd bought it, or at least that was the story I made up based on the keys dangling from Stella's hand. Stella and her partner looked similar: tall, willowy women in reflective sunglasses, smiling authentic smiles. "That's Marianne," Stella said sweetly.

I don't know why my face got hot then. I should have

said something—even one word would have been good—
but I froze instead.

"Are you okay?" Stella asked.

"Do you mind if I use your bathroom?"

"Of course," she said.

I didn't actually have to go to the bathroom, so I just
closed the door and stood there. I stared at the button on
top of the toilet and mentally prepared to press it after the
correct amount of time had passed. And then I remembered
the thing I often remember in bathrooms, which is how
much time I used to spend throwing up. In my most recent
apartment in San Francisco, I had a whole system for ar-
ranging towels around the base so my knees wouldn't hurt. I
really thought that was genius when I made it up.

I turned to look in the mirror.

Who are you now?

And then, I don't know why—maybe to torture myself,
or maybe to remind myself—I pulled my shirt up and forced
myself to look at the scar, which ran from my shoulder blade
to my waist and was shaped like a wisp. That's what I always
thought when I saw it. Wisp. It curved to match the twisted
piece of metal I'd flown into on Van Ness.

Bam, the car hits me.

Bam, I fly into a twisted piece of metal.

Slice, the keepsake of a scar.

What about now?

I flushed the toilet, then turned on the faucet and pretended to wash my hands. Stella and Marianne had matching Sonicare toothbrushes and used organic toothpaste.
Aesop hand soap and lotion. Lip balm called Hurraw! I

made a mental note of these products. I always did this when I encountered people I admired. Some part of me must have thought that if I owned what they owned and dressed the way they dressed, then possibly I could become them.

Back downstairs, Stella and I set a date and picked a time, and I laid out a plan.

"It's always best to start with the hardest thing," I said like this was a firm rule I believed in, which I guess I did. "In your case, it's the papers. We'll start there, and then we'll move on to the clothes."

"That sounds perfect," Stella said, and I believed her. If Stella thought it was perfect, then it probably was.

In the doorway, we said all the things.

"Thank you," "so nice to meet you," "see you soon," "I can't wait."

And after we'd said all the things, Stella hugged me warmly, so warmly that I almost wanted to cry, and then I was moving, at first backward and then forward down her curved walkway on numb legs. I glanced down at my feet several times, amazed at how they continued to do their job.

Even when you feel like you have no idea who you are or where you're going, your body kind of knows for you.

CHAPTER 6

stevie

As I drove home from Stella's, I had a thought that I often have while driving around La Jolla: *I cannot believe I came back here.*

Before we move on with this story, I need to tell you about what happened six months ago. But in order to understand what happened six months ago, you need a quick rundown of what I'd been doing for the twenty years before that.

In a nutshell, I'd been moving. You know that book *Wherever You Go, There You Are*?

I know that book, too. I bought it for myself several times in the hopes that I'd get the memo.

But then I kept not getting the memo.

When I left La Jolla at eighteen, it was with a vengeance. *See you never again.* La Jolla was the site of my problems. It was the memory of my pain. It was also a culture-less monster in a pretty dress, and I didn't want pretty anymore. I wanted gritty. I wanted ugly. Thankfully, most places are uglier than La Jolla, so it wasn't that hard to achieve this goal.

My first destination was supposed to be Stanford, but it was not. I went to UC Santa Cruz instead, where four years shot by me like a cannonball. I don't remember a lot, and what I do remember, I try to forget. I did drugs I hadn't heard of then and haven't heard of since. AMT? What is that? I still don't know.

One night, I bought a peyote cactus ear from a guy named Stash for twenty bucks. He gave it to me in a plastic Safeway bag. Alone in my campus apartment, when none of my six suitemates were home, I dethorned, blended, and drank it. Nothing happened. I then ordered a pizza from Domino's, ate it all, and fell asleep on top of the giant stuffed elephant my roommate had won at a fair, and honestly, I was probably thinking about Chris. I thought about her a lot, but I never called her, and she never called me either.

After Santa Cruz, I got a job at a newspaper in San Francisco, a terrible job for which I was paid nothing, not that it mattered. Mom was paying for everything anyway. I didn't have to work, but I wanted to. Working meant that I was functioning. Working meant that I was not my father. After a few months at the paper, I quit and got my first job at a bar, where I could drink too much without being judged. I started blacking out a lot and sleeping with weird men. I tried not to, but it kept happening.

So I moved to New York. I worked at another bar. I slept with more weird men. Then, during a brutal winter, I slept with a weird woman. In the morning she said, "I like you," and smiled at me slyly, as if we'd known each other for much longer than eight hours. On her bedside table was a framed photo of a black cat, the same black cat that was curled up between us in her bed. She had red silk sheets and a luxury apartment on Central Park West. Once, she'd been a dancer. Now she drank gin during the day. She kept coming to the bar to see me after that night, and it was too much.

So I got in my car and drove to Florida, where at least it would be warm. I chain-smoked Parliament Lights the whole way, and didn't stop until I reached the Keys, only because the continent ended there. If it hadn't, I would have kept driving forever.

In the Keys, I rented a cottage on the beach and got a job at a hotel bar and switched from vodka to whiskey because it seemed like a more refined choice. I watched the sunset every night, trying to find meaning in the gently glowing Creamsicle swirls of the Florida sky. Every time someone walked by me on the beach, I reminded myself that to them, I was just a woman having one drink. Just a woman having one proper drink while enjoying her sunset, and it was fine. I'd wave. I'd smile. I'd think, *Tomorrow I will go to Pilates.* Then I'd get drunk.

One night I went out and woke up on the beach about a mile from my cottage. My mouth was bleeding. My jaw hurt. I didn't know what had happened to me, but I did know that I couldn't trust myself anymore. The cottage, the hotel bar, and trips to Publix to buy liquor and groceries became my small world.

I lied to Mom on the phone.

"Yes, I'm glad to be here," I told her. "No, I'm not lonely."

"Do you want to come home for a visit?"

"No thanks."

Mom was always inviting me home, and I was always declining. Over a span of twenty years, I returned to La Jolla maybe ten times. Before every visit, I promised myself I wouldn't drink too much. Then I drank too much. Mom never said anything, even though I'm sure she noticed.

Anyway, shortly after the morning I woke up on the beach in Florida, I realized I needed to move again. But this time, I needed more than a new city. I needed a new country. So I went to Paris and worked as a freelancer, copyediting a British woman's blog about makeup, making sure there were *U*s in places they didn't belong. (Blog post example: "My Favourite Concealer!") It was unnatural, and then it grew unbearable, so I quit.

Then I moved again.

And got another job.

And quit again.

And moved again.

And it kept going like this.

I was addicted to a fresh start. The soundtrack of my life was the manic rip of zippers gliding violently back and forth. Opening, closing, starting, ending, hello, goodbye. *Goodbye* was my middle name, although in reality, I didn't have one. So technically my middle name was *Nonexistent*, which fit, too. I was a noncommittal guest star in a lot of people's lives. I blew into town—hello!—and then blew out. Goodbye.

Every time I arrived in a new city and found a new apartment, I wanted it to be different, and it was, until I settled in and made it the same: a Spartan box, as modern as possible, with a toilet to throw up in. In some cities I got lazy and used my suitcase as a dresser, but normally, when I arrived in a new place, I'd buy a new dresser, sometimes two, plus a bed and a desk and a shower curtain and everything else. I reveled in the setting-up phase. I'd go to the store and carefully consider how each piece of furniture matched my personality or didn't. Was *this* me? Was *this*? My decoration identity went through frequent and dramatic changes. Because in every new city, I thought, *Here, I will be completely different than I was there. Here, I will become my true self, the self that I was meant to be all along.*

For a while, I could sustain the delusion that I was on the verge of becoming my true self. Then I'd hit a moment of clarity. In retrospect, it was more like the desire for clarity rather than clarity itself—a false wall—but whatever, it was better than nothing. In those moments, I'd open my eyes and think, *This is not working.* My head would be splitting open, and no amount of Advil could save me. I'd lay a cold, wet washcloth over my forehead and make a new plan. The new plan was always the same: quit the bad job and leave the bad city and ditch everything I'd bought that reminded me of bad times. I'd get rid of my furniture. I'd get rid of the apartment. I'd say goodbye again.

The scenery kept changing, but my regrets remained the same. I was obsessed with moment when it had all gone wrong, the moment that turned out to be the difference between the life I wanted to be living and the life I was accidentally living instead. If only I hadn't gone over to Chris's house that night, then I would have won, and gotten into Stanford, and secured a big job, and—whatever, I wasn't sure about all the details, but the point is that it would have been great.

———————

By thirty-six, I had nothing to show for my run so far on this earth besides passport stamps and a bunch of names in my phone that I didn't recognize and a body that was becoming increasingly mangled. Often, I'd find a new bruise and have no idea where it came from. Often, I'd forget where I lived. When you're stumbling around drunk at night, all cities look the same.

I'd been living in Atlanta for four or five months when I saw the Golden Gate Bridge in a car commercial. I thought it was a sign that I should move back to San Francisco, because like all lost people, I was constantly looking for signs.

I arrived a few days later, ready for a fresh start. I found an apartment, I bought furniture, I got a job at a bar.

Then the accident happened. Mom wanted to fly up to see me, but I told her not to. "It's not a big deal," I said. "Just a bad coincidence." I mean, yes, it sucked to get hit by a car, and it wasn't fun to land on a jagged shard of metal either, which was actually a piece of another car, probably from a previous accident, that was lying in an empty lot. What were the chances of that happening?

I didn't really mind spending a few weeks in the hospital. I'd been needing a break anyway. I turned thirty-seven while

I was there, and the nurses brought a cake, and honestly, it was kind of nice.

I went back to my old life after that. The only difference was that I was more careful when crossing the street. Otherwise, it was the same. I returned to the bar job. I kept drinking. I ate lots of three a.m. burritos.

And then one morning, everything changed.

I woke up next to a strange man.

On his neck was a birthmark the shape of a country that I couldn't quite place.

"Stevie," he said.

I couldn't quite place the man's name either. Was it John? Jim? I didn't respond.

When I sat up in his bed to look for my clothes, he said, "Hey, what happened to your back?"

I didn't answer him. I found my clothes, some of which were in the bathroom, and I left without saying goodbye.

On the walk back to my apartment, I listened to a voicemail from my mom.

"The house sold! I know you don't want to come down here, but I could really use your help with the move. I would ask Bonnie, but she's in Hawaii with Dwight. You know, their yearly reconnection thing. Anyway, you're the best packer I know! And I want you to come see this cute place I bought down at the Shores. Please? It'll only take a few weeks."

I stopped walking. Because I was out of breath and walking up a hill.

And then it hit me.

I hated hills. I hated fog. I turned around. The sunlight

GETTING CLEAN WITH STEVIE GREEN   43

spotted the city like a skin disorder. Beyond the buildings the ocean was gray.

What happened to your back?

I hated San Francisco.

Mom had been begging me to come home ever since I got out of the hospital. And I kept saying no. On any other day, I would have said no again. But on this day, in this moment, looking at this city, I couldn't think of anything better to do than leave.

———

When Mom started talking about selling the house on Moonridge Drive, I didn't think she was serious, even though it was very clearly the right thing to do. For years I'd said, "That house is too big for one person," but Mom said she didn't care. "Dad and I bought this house together. I refuse to let it go."

Dad had now been dead for thirty-four years.

And Mom, for thirty-four years, had been clutched to his memory like a stone in the pocket.

But the house had problems, and Mom was sick of dealing with them. The pool needed to be retiled. The walls needed to be repainted. The fence needed to be rebuilt. The maintenance was a full-time job, and Mom was over it. Really, she'd always been over it, and that's why the house had a Grey Gardens feel. She was good at living with problems until they became painful to her, and her threshold for pain was high.

Then two things happened. One, a tree fell onto the roof, and two, when Mom went out to the yard to assess the problem, she tripped and broke her foot and suddenly became aware of her own mortality. "I'm sixty-seven and I just realized I'm not going to live forever." When she went to the doctor to get her foot fixed, she learned that she had shrunk, from five feet five to five feet four. So on top of feeling broken and mortal, she was also disappearing, inch by little inch. "Now that I'm smaller, I can see that this house is too big," she said, and I stopped myself from saying, *I've been telling you that for years*, even though I wanted to. Instead I just said, "Yes."

It only took me two days to disassemble my San Francisco life. I called the landlord and told him I was leaving. "I'm moving to Berlin," I said, because that's where I was planning to go after the short trip back to La Jolla. I put all my stuff out on the street. I booked a flight. During the plane ride, I had no deep thoughts. I was just tired.

Mom was overjoyed when she picked me up at the airport. "I'm so happy you're here!"

"Me too," I said, even though it was a lie. I had no intention of being anything close to happy during this trip.

But then an expected thing happened. As we veered off the 5, the sight of the pretty green hills was pleasant to me rather than irritating, and the smells of salt air and eucalyptus reminded me of how I'd felt as a young child, before things went south.

I'd been happy here once.

My reaction surprised me, although maybe it shouldn't have. What was home besides, inevitably, home? What was

more comforting than familiarity? I know that the only reason I was asking these questions was because I was so tired.
I'd been in a hole my entire adult life, digging deeper and
deeper, and suddenly I was too tired to keep digging, and I
was lying down on the ground, and I was looking up at the
dot of sky above me, probably hoping to be saved.

———————

Mom and I started going through her stuff the day after I
arrived, and I quickly became the boss.

"Stevie, what do you think?" she would ask, holding up
some old thing she'd doodled on, and I would say, "Yes or
no? Be honest." This was the system I used for myself every
time I moved, but I'd never really told anyone about it. It
just seemed too obvious to say out loud. What other possible options were there, besides yes and no?

Moonridge was and still is the biggest job I've ever done,
both because of the massive downsize it included and because it was personal—and personalized. My mother saw the
tangible world as one great big canvas. She drew on everything she owned. Every table, every chair, every oven mitt.
Everything. If an earring had a surface large enough to draw
on, then she had drawn on it. If she had an idea that she
couldn't express in words, then it was probably depicted on
one of her walls.

Since Mom was an artist—well-known in La Jolla for
her intricate dolls—this passed for the good kind of insan-
ity rather than the plainly insane kind, but either way,
Mom's argument sounded insane. "But I drew on it, so it's
art now."

This led to many long and annoying discussions, during which we tried to answer the question, *What is art?*

Was art a shoe rack Mom had covered in red stars with a felt-tip marker ten years earlier, a broomstick she'd wrapped in fluorescent orange masking tape, or a pair of my sister, Bonnie's, shoes from childhood, now imprinted with hundreds of cursive *B*'s?

And what about the famous apple pie from the Julian Bakery that she'd burned to ashes by accident five Thanksgivings earlier? It now took up a prominent place on the sculpture shelf. Because now it was a sculpture, and, according to Mom, a rare one. "How many people do you think have one of these at home?"

I assured Mom that she could burn another pie at the new place. She relented. We threw it out. And it kept going like this. Mom, unsure; me, the voice of reason.

The hardest part of move was, as expected, Mom's attachment to the ghost of my dead dad. Initially, she refused to part with anything that even remotely reminded her of him. She wanted to keep every picture, every object he'd ever bought, and every item she remembered him touching. "I think he read some of that book," she said about a copy of Milan Kundera's *The Unbearable Lightness of Being*.

"Dad was a loser," I reminded her. "He couldn't even finish a book! You deserve so much more! You need to start dating!"

In response to my yelling, Mom usually left the room. Over time, I got quieter, which led to improved results. Once she even said, "Okay, and *how* would I start dating?"

But before I could answer, she backtracked. "No, never mind."

So Mom wasn't ready to make progress in some areas. But she made great progress in others. Somehow—and I thought this was a miracle—she eventually said goodbye to everything that reminded her of Dad, minus three photos and the red urn containing his ashes.

"Can we spread those, please?"

"Not yet."

"It's been thirty-four years."

"I'm not ready."

The urn and the photos now lived on a ledge in Mom's bedroom along with some feathers and rocks. It looked like an altar, and I still thought it was a waste of space, but I didn't tell her that. Instead I focused on the positive. "Mom, I'm so proud of all your progress."

I said this a lot during the move, because it was true. And I was more than proud, really. I was in awe. I'd never expected my mother to leave that house, or to get rid of so much stuff. Every time she said no to another item, I reminded her of how proud I was, and she said, "I couldn't be doing this without you, Stevie."

At first, I didn't expect my presence to be so valuable. Mom could have just asked herself the question. But I soon realized that it wasn't only about the question. It was about emotions, and Mom's were getting in the way of her decision-making abilities. She needed a witness. I needed a sense of purpose. And now I had one.

A week in, Mom said, "You haven't been drinking."

"I guess I'm taking a break," I told her.

After I said it out loud, my break felt more official, and I decided to take a break from smoking, too. I threw my Parliament Lights in the trash can and drizzled them with dish detergent to prevent myself from trying to retrieve them later, which I'd done a million times before. I had this sense—it was somehow both vague and pinching at the same time—that if I didn't change now, I probably never would.

The more days I went without getting drunk, the better I felt. I mean, I know that sounds like a ridiculous thing to say, but it was a revelation to me. I felt high on real life. I started eating healthier. I went running on the beach for the first time. I cut all my hair off, and I felt infinitely lighter. The idea of moving to Berlin began to seem less appealing. Also, Mom had already begun planting her seeds. "You're very good at this, Stevie. You should start a business." At some point she asked, "What would it be like if you stayed?"

Then she told me what it would be like: "It would be, like, the best thing ever! You can have the main house down at the Shores and I'll take the pool house. And I'll buy you a car, same as mine. We can have matching cars!" Also, she'd tell all her friends to hire me. "Plus, I read that loneliness kills people. You wouldn't want me to die of loneliness, would you?"

I didn't surrender to Mom's plan because it was the right thing to do, or because she was sixty-seven and shrinking. I did it because I was out of options. And I'd been given just enough hope. I liked the idea of starting my own business. It seemed so perfectly meta. I'd use my obsession with renewal to help other people and in the process, be renewed myself. Eventually, I would come to feel like the inside of a decluttered house, like all the parts of me had been organized in a way that wasn't so uncomfortable.

CHAPTER 7

stevie

Mom was out front eating a breadstick when I got home, which should have been my clue that something was off. Who sits in front of their house eating a breadstick? Also, it was an hour before dinnertime.

Since moving to the Shores, Mom and I had formed some pretty cute routines together, and the main one was dinner. Every night at six thirty, we ate by the pool between our two houses on some of the patio furniture we'd brought over from Moonridge. Our setup included a round table with four chairs and an umbrella for the sun. The table used to be clear, but Mom had colored in the bubbles of glass mosaic-style, so it was now an outburst of reds and blues and yellows. "Morocco-meets-the-kindergarten-classroom" was how she described it.

Using the same so-simple-it's-either-dumb-or-genius system we'd used to declutter Moonridge—*Is this a yes or a no?*—Mom and I were currently in the midst of revolutionizing other elements of our lives. Everything was about clarity now. Everything we'd never stopped to question was now up for debate. Mom had always cooked because that's what people did, but did she *like* cooking? No. Neither did I, and therefore we decided to be modern people who ordered takeout instead. We also decided that we liked each other's company. So, family dinner.

Mom had given me the bigger of the two houses at the Shores so that I could turn one of the bedrooms into an office, which I'd done. I bought a wide bamboo desk and an extra chair for the assistant I planned to hire one day. The house, like Mom's, had a white stucco exterior and a Spanish tile roof, and the thing I liked about it most was that it made me feel held, but loosely, which was how I thought an ideal clutter-free space should make you feel: loosely held, like you were cupped in the relaxed palm of the universe, one that never threatened to curl its fist around you. It was cozy, but airy. And just in case it wasn't airy enough, I left all the windows a millimeter open. I hated to feel boxed in.

I'd decorated the interior as sparsely as possible. Minus a few accent pieces—gray pillows on the couch, an oil painting with a lot of yellow in it, the red teakettle I'd bought because I liked the style and no other colors were available—everything else was white, white, white. *No color, no thank you* was the message of my house and of my wardrobe.

Thanks to an epiphany I'd had upon awakening from a nap—*Oh my god, I can just say no to color, period*—I now only wore black and white. This made shopping so much easier because it shrank the list of options down to almost nothing. I often thought about how I'd wasted so much time being confused about stupid things, like whether I should buy a sweater in purple or red. Now, if I liked a sweater, I just bought it in both black and in white and I was done.

Restrictions, contrary to what many people think, are the real definition of freedom.

Life at the Shores was going well, maybe even better than expected. I liked living so close to the beach, and Mom liked her little pool house. She said its tiny size made her feel like she was back in the womb, where she began. "I don't miss all that space," she said. "I'm anti-space now." What she did miss about Moonridge were the Monterey cypress trees, because Dad had planted them, and the decrepit blue garden shed, because Dad had painted it blue.

I should probably tell you that since my dad died when I was three years old, I'd never really known him. I don't remember him dying. I don't remember feeling sad that he was gone. Yes, as an adult, I might have felt like something essential was missing from my life, but was it my father? Weren't people always talking about how they felt like they were missing something? Didn't everyone, if they were being honest, have the sense that they were full of holes?

"How did your dad die?"

When people asked me this question, I usually just said cancer. It was easier than telling the real story.

My single memory of Dad: He's drinking a beer in the yard on a sunny day. His head's tipped back, but his sombrero magically stays on. I'm not sure if this memory is real or not, though. It might be a memory of a photo.

I'd been sitting in the car for five minutes now, peering through the slim opening in the hedge at Mom nibbling her breadstick, and checking my phone, too, obviously, as everybody is doing all the time. Chris Dane was not on Instagram. Neither was Brad Rose. I already knew these facts, but I double-checked them again just to make sure.

And then I got out of the car, and as I walked toward my mother, I was thinking about how fully she embodied the caricature of herself as the Doll Lady, as she was known colloquially to some. This evening's ensemble included an explosion of mismatched textures and hues: light green spandex leggings, an almond-brown crocheted sweater, a sparkly purple scarf.

She hadn't noticed me walking toward her yet.

Then I stepped on some crunchy leaves and she whipped around. "Aaah! You scared me!" She bolted to standing like a flustered criminal and chucked the stub of her breadstick onto the front hedge.

"Mo-om," I sang in a jokingly accusatory tone, the subtext of which could have either been (a) *What are you hiding?* or (b) *Throwing food at a plant is not the same as composting.* I'd told her this many times and her response was always the same: "It's all nature."

Yes, it was all nature, but it also made our front hedge look like trash. Mom's breadstick hadn't made it through the crevices, but remained on top instead, totally visible. Below it, the remains of last week's pad thai dangled from the leaves like calcified tinsel. An ornamental dumpling we'd ordered over a month earlier was still lodged between the branches.

I kissed her cheek, then looked at her sideways. "You're acting guilty. What did you do?"

She batted her eyes in a sketchy way and shifted her

weight evenly into both feet. Re-grounding was a nervous
tic she'd picked up at yoga. Then she opened her mouth, but
before she could say anything, the side gate creaked open
and out ran—

"Wiener?"

Wiener was my sister, Bonnie's, dachshund.

"What's *Wiener* doing here?"

I hadn't seen Bonnie in three months and three weeks,
not that anyone was counting.

"Umm," Mom began.

"Is *Bonnie* here?"

Bonnie had been avoiding me like the plague our whole
adult lives, and I still didn't understand why.

CHAPTER 8

stevie

Dinner was tense.

Bonnie downed her wine and didn't look at me. I wasn't hungry and didn't look at her either. Mom gently stabbed her pesto rotini and said, "Since my house is so small, Stevie, we were hoping that Bonnie could live with you for a while."

"How long is 'a while'?" I asked, eyeing the dump site of Bonnie's things that had formed on the other side of the pool. There were suitcases and boxes and bags exploding with clothes, at least three unforgivably hideous lamps, a few surfboards, a grimy Hula-Hoop, and a random stack of papers. Wiener's dog bed, which had been designed to look like an onion bagel, was perched precariously over the edge of a box.

"I don't know," Bonnie whimpered, holding her wineglass up for Mom to refill. Even this small gesture seemed hard for her to accomplish right now. Her arm lifted with the energy of a soaked beach towel: heavy, put-upon, and unlike its usual sun-affiliated self.

What you need to know is that my sister and I had nothing in common. She was a redhead. My hair was blond. She'd been labeled "chill." I'd been labeled "the high-maintenance one." Her needs were few. I had a long list of needs, each one accompanied by a box that yearned to be checked soon. Bonnie, like Mom, didn't take naturally to routines. She lived by the seat of her pants and let the wind blow her to her next destination and always arrived late. I checked my watch often, wore a windbreaker for the wind, and arrived five minutes early to all events. Bonnie wore her life like a billowing kaftan. I wore mine like a speed-enhancing leotard.

Bonnie believed in invisible things, like rock crystals, palm readings, and the magic of essential oils that had been chanted to by a bald YouTube shaman from Colorado. I believed in all that stuff, too, because I was as woo-woo as anyone else who'd grown up in Southern California, but more than anything, I believed in productivity, in the harmonious dance of input and output. Bonnie didn't give a shit about productivity. She was a lazy sprig drifting through the universe, and I was a relentlessly built brick wall, with each brick lined up just so. I must have thought in some essential way that life was designed to be difficult. Bonnie seemed to think it was a coast down a bunny slope followed by French onion soup at the chalet, and so it was for her: a consistent unfolding of wonderful accidents. When she was thirteen, a random kid in Cardiff had lent her a surfboard and she'd become a surfer. Her long-term relationship with Dwight had begun on their very first day at UCSD, when Bonnie's flip-flop became entangled with his in the auditorium during freshman orientation.

Bonnie had had three serious boyfriends in her life, all with the worst names: Carl, Rob, Dwight. Apart from short breaks between these relationships, she'd never been single. To boyfriends, to surfing, to her dog, and to tacos, Bonnie was deeply committed. But to all endeavors involving the exchange of money, she was the person who'd ghost you. She was basically a professional hobbyist. This was the problem when you weren't forced to work for money. It zapped your drive.

It didn't zap your ability to be Insta-famous, however. Bonnie's passions made for a very appealing page that had earned her 22,232 followers the last time I'd checked. To strangers, she looked like a lifestyle brand, a quintessentially Californian one that fit into the standard fantasy of what it was like to live here. The surfing played a big role in that, and her red hair made her just a little bit different—but not too different. She was a twinge quirky, pretty but not stunning, and it never seemed like she was trying too hard because she genuinely wasn't.

Bonnie's natural appeal was a draw, but that's not the only reason she was Insta-famous. She was obsessed with taking pictures and always had been, which meant that she had tons of material to choose from when it came to filling the square. Also, unlike me, she understood the game. She was a master of the filter and the hashtag and all the other details that I was only just learning about.

But while Bonnie might have been selling the image of a maximum life on Instagram, in reality, she had no direction and she had no drive. She was the beaver who did the back-float, and I was the beaver building the entire dam myself, and this was what worried me about us living together. I could already see one of her nachos staining my spotless white interior.

Was I envious of Bonnie's leaf-fell-in-my-water-and-that's-how-tea-was-invented style?

Probably.

Was I pissed at her for avoiding me?

Yes.

After I'd moved back to La Jolla, I thought we might become friends again. Short of that, I at least expected her to have coffee with me every once in a while, but she kept saying no. She was hell-bent on evading my requests to hang out, as she'd been doing forever. I'd invited her over five times, and every time, she'd rejected me with a lame excuse. *I have to walk Wiener. Dwight and I are going to Oregon to buy cheese.*

It had taken all my best brain cells to not say, *Who goes to Oregon to buy cheese?*

Bonnie had only appeared twice at the Shores since Mom and I had moved in, and on both occasions, it was while I wasn't home.

"You just missed her," Mom said twice.

"How convenient," I responded twice.

And now I was being asked to *live* with her?

On the one hand, I wanted to scream, *You've treated me like a stranger for years and now you want to move in? No!*

But on the other hand, what I wanted—in the depths of my heart, the really deep depths, where the rawest feelings you had as a baby live—was for us to be friends again.

There was no way in hell I was going to admit to that,

though. I also didn't know if a friendship was possible. Maybe we'd grown too far apart, and a reunion was unrealistic. Maybe our differences were irreconcilable.

It took me a long moment to gather myself. Then I realized that the woman I wanted to be would have said, "Of *course* you can live with me for a while, Bonnie." So I went with that.

Bonnie's usual brightness resurfaced. For a moment, she radiated. "Thank you, oh my god, thank you!" she exclaimed, pawing my arm. "And Wiener, too, right?"

Hearing his name, the little black sausage unfurled himself and started wagging the knobby cord of his tail, which was really nothing more than an extension of his spine wrapped in fur. "He only weighs eight pounds, and he'll never poop inside," she promised.

Mom, correctly sensing how uncool this was, offered a suggestion. "Or Weenie could be an outside dog now."

"And get eaten by coyotes?" Bonnie looked at Mom, repulsed, then nuzzled her face between Wiener's ears and said something unintelligible.

"I'm going to ask an obvious question," I said. "What happened to Dwight?"

At this, Bonnie's demeanor dimmed again. Then she started to cry. I handed her my napkin and wished my emotions would come out in a torrential downpour like hers did, but only every few months and only when I was alone.

Several bites of my salad later, she had regrouped. She blew her nose at least three times. Wiener didn't move. He seemed used to her mood shifts. Finally, in a snotty voice, she delivered the news. "Dwight met some bitch in the desert."

"A young healer," Mom chimed in. "Yvonne. She's eighteen. They're going to Peru to do an ayahuasca ceremony, which I think sounds rather intriguing."

"You know they make you barf first," Bonnie said angrily. She drank more wine, which didn't look delicious to me at all, then explained how she'd deluded herself into thinking that she and Dwight were the happiest they'd ever been. Now she could see her delusion for what it was.

Exhibit one: the list they'd written together and taped on the fridge, which Bonnie now excavated from inside the kangaroo pouch of the Mexican poncho she'd bought in Portland a hundred years earlier and hadn't taken off since. It was the color of a faded butterscotch candy with light purple stripes, and its McDonald's-red hood, when it was on, made her head look like a warning button. The disaster of this poncho, along with Bonnie's puka-shell necklace and her *Annie* hair, made her impossible to lose in a crowd. They were her signature things. They shouted, *YO, I'M BONNIE!*

She uncrumpled the list, which had been ripped up and then remorsefully taped back together. "This is so I can remember how delusional I am." She sighed, then read:

"We are healthy.
Wiener is healthy.
We have a GREAT house.
We live in SAN DIEGO.
We attend three cultural events per month.
We sleep for eight hours most nights.
We have EACH OTHER!"

Bonnie re-crumpled the list and stuffed it back inside her pouch. "I wrote it a week ago, when Dwight was still in the desert."

I phrased my statement as if it were a question so it would come across as nonjudgmental. "I thought you wrote it together?"

Bonnie yanked the hood of her poncho over her head and frowned. "We were on the phone. He called me from his yurt."

"Turtledove," Mom began, her merry tone somehow both warm and dismissive at once, "you need to get a little part-time job. It'll take your mind off things."

Bonnie swigged her wine. "I can't right now. I have nothing to give. Plus, what would I do? I was wrong about becoming a chef, acupuncture school was a hoax, and I *hate* the bead store."

If there was a common theme among Bonnie's professions—chef, acupuncturist, bead-store clerk—it was that they'd all begun and ended with fervent enthusiasm. Before hating the bead store, she'd told Mom—who'd then told me—that beading with your homies on a Friday night was going to be the new ceramic café. Bonnie loved beads. She adored beads. She could not get enough beads. Then— *bam!*—she *hated* the bead store. After getting fired for being late too many times.

Bonnie was like this with everything: either all in or all out. Her feelings flipped like a switch.

Bam!

Bonnie might have been erratic, but at least she was decisive. She always knew exactly what she wanted. So when she made the following statement, Mom and I exchanged a look of genuine concern.

"The only thing I've been sure about for the last seventeen years is that Dwight is my soul mate, and now it turns out I was wrong about that. I could be wrong about everything. I don't know who I am right now."

I was staring at Mom's pearlescent face when the idea struck her. Her eyes shot open. With a mad gleam in her eye, she pointed a finger at me and wagged it up and down, nodding along to her plan, which she laid out in a series of three distinct and manipulative parts: ask question, acquire answer, present solution.

1. Mom: "Stevie, didn't you tell me you need an assistant?"
2. Me: "Oh god."
3. Mom: "Hire Bonnie!"

My jaw clenched. My fingers curled into themselves. I glared at my mother. *How could you do this to me?*

Letting Bonnie live with me was already worrisome. I'd already replayed her future nacho staining my spotless white interior at least fourteen times since I'd originally envisioned it. And adding Wiener to the mix was a huge compromise, especially considering he wasn't even hypoallergenic—but I couldn't say no or he might get eaten by a coyote, in which case Bonnie, given her codependent nature, would probably die ten days after his funeral. All of this was already very bad. But hiring my sister to be my organizing partner? For my clients, it would be like going to the dentist and being told by the hygienist, *I'm actually a professional doorman and I've never scraped plaque before, but you should trust me anyway.*

I pumped my clenched fists, trying to come up with a generous response.

But I failed.

I failed hard.

Actually, I was screaming.

"Bonnie? As my assistant? Are you kidding? She's a mess!"

I told myself to stop, then kept going. "And that poncho smells like old re-microwaved French fries."

Bonnie sniffed her sleeve. "I *like* the smell of French fries!"

"Calm, children, calm." Mom patted down the air around her with both hands. "It's my dying wish for you to work together. You used to be so close."

"Nobody's dying, Mom," I said, annoyed.

"Everybody's dying," Bonnie groaned.

Mom uncrossed her legs and set her feet evenly on the ground. "Babies," she began, "who pays your bills? Who bought your cars? Whose property is this?"

Silence.

"But Mom!" I was a door-slamming teenager again. "How am I ever going to become La Jolla's number one de-cluttering guru with Bonnie as my sidekick?"

For good measure, I gave Bonnie's landfill a long, hard stare. Wiener's bagel-inspired dog bed was now upside down on the ground, and some of her papers had blown into the pool.

"Like I can control the wind!" Bonnie argued energetically, although she apparently didn't have the energy to get up and fetch her papers with the net that was right there.

"Oh, come *on*, Stevie." Mom slapped my arm playfully. "You've always been very resourceful."

I glared at my mother again. My nostrils flared.

She winked at me in a way that said, *Do me this favor.*

I took a deep breath. Or I didn't, but I thought about it. I tried to accept my fate. Then I tried to rig this nightmare in my favor. "Fine," I said. "But I reserve the right to fire Bonnie at any time."

"Fair," Mom said, her fist gaveling the table.

Bonnie unleashed her hands from her pouch and pointed two finger-guns at me. "I didn't want to work for you anyway, but now I kind of do since you don't think I can!"

How could I have overlooked that my sister the contrarian would be enlivened by the chance to fight? A refusal inspired Bonnie more than anything. Many of her most notable pursuits had been unearthed only because someone had told her she was incapable of pursuing them. The real reason she'd started surfing was because that kid in Cardiff who'd lent her the board had said, "Bet you can't catch *one* wave."

"You don't think I can handle cleaning up rich people's crap so they can tell all their friends they've participated in some stupid New Age fad that forces them to get rid of stuff, but is really just an excuse to go shopping?"

"See Mom? She doesn't get it." I turned to Bonnie. "And no, of course I don't think you can do it. You've never had a job for longer than two months."

"Oh, really?" Bonnie said. "What's the longest you've ever had a job? You can't even live in the same city for more than a year and a half!"

"I'm different now," I said. "And this isn't just a job. It's my *business*."

"Honestly, Bon." Mom spoke with so much love in her voice that it would take us all a moment to process the fact that what came next wasn't very nice. "I don't think you can do it either, but it's worth a shot."

Bonnie's eyes popped open so rabidly that I thought she might start foaming at the mouth. "I'm going to prove both of you wrong."

Of course I didn't believe her, and I could tell Mom didn't either.

"If you're going to work for me," I said, motioning to the poncho, "I require that you throw that thing in the trash and get a total and complete makeover."

Bonnie gave me a quick once-over. "I'm not going to dress like Inspector Gadget, the Oreo Cookie Edition, if that's what you're hoping for."

"Bonnie?" I returned her eye sweep. "You look like you just rolled out of a hot-boxed van."

"You're perfect and I'm a slob. Got it." Bonnie turned her palm to touch the imaginary wall between us and faced the other way. In middle school, this had been code for *Talk to the hand*, and really, it was the most apt gesture she could have made, because it felt like we were suddenly back in middle school.

Mom's opinions about Bonnie's appearance took the form of a gentle stabbing motion, which was the same motion she was using to gather pasta off her plate. First, the gentleness: "Bonnie, I love you." Then, the stab: "But unfortunately, Stevie's right about your appearance. You can't be a professional organizer in those clothes."

Bonnie braced herself, clutching onto her nasty poncho like it was a life raft. "This was a *gift*."

"From whom?" Mom asked.

"Dwight."

Mom displayed no judgment on her face. This was another thing she'd learned at yoga. "Bonnie," she said evenly, "we're taking you to the mall. It's time to get rid of that poncho. Dwight wasn't good enough for you anyway."

"What?" Bonnie was horrified. "You didn't like Dwight?"

"I would never say that." Mom stood. *"Vámonos!"*

"You didn't like Dwight for *seventeen* years and you never told me?"

Mom ignored Bonnie and glanced at Wiener, who was chasing the tip of his spinal cord in circles. "Wiener will be fine out here by the pool for an hour."

"After you get back," I said, "you can pull out the couch bed in the office. I'll put sheets in there for you."

"Chop, chop," Mom said. "The mall is waiting."

"The *mall*," Bonnie repeated with disdain.

"And work starts tomorrow at eight," I said. "Be dressed."

CHAPTER 9

kit

My thirty-five-year-old child put her feet up on the dash like she was ten and said, "I can't believe you and Stevie got matching cars."

"Do you want one? I'll get you one, too."

Of course I understood that you weren't supposed to spoil your children, but it was too late. My children were already spoiled. Have you ever heard of a rotten banana coming back to life?

After Jack's death, I had no choice but to spoil them. I thought of my credit card as a guilty conscience in action. I didn't tell Bonnie and Stevie the truth about how Jack died until they were fourteen and sixteen. I thought that when I did, I would feel less guilty, but it didn't turn out that way. Stevie started drinking more. I thought it was my fault. So what did I do? I bought them more things.

What's the point of having money if you aren't going to spend it?

This was the line I fed myself when I worried that I'd failed at motherhood.

"I don't want a car," Bonnie said. "I just feel left out. You guys are, like, in a rhythm. And Stevie *hates* me."

"She doesn't *hate* you," I said.

"She can't even look at me."

"Listen. You're going to show up and be the most giving employee you can be. Stevie would never admit it, but she really needs your help."

"She does?"

"Yes, she does. And you can't run off in a few months because you're bored, Bonnie. You have to stick with this, okay?"

Bonnie sighed. "Do you think Dwight's going to come back to me?"

"Honestly, Bon? I hope not. Dwight is . . . like wallpaper. Just there."

"Just *there*?" Bonnie said. "*How* could you not have told me this before, Mom?"

"You wouldn't have heard me."

"What else are you not telling me?"

That I think I've made your life too easy and now you don't know how to try and I'm sorry, that I'm worried you have no sense of yourself outside a relationship, that I fear dying before you're ready to handle it.

"Nothing that I can think of right now," I said.

CHAPTER 10

stevie

Would it surprise you to learn that I am a person who thrives on routine? Would it surprise you to learn that if my routine is derailed in any way, I feel like my life is spinning out of control?

A rough outline of my days:

Coffee

Work out

Work

Lunch

More Coffee

Work

Work

Dinner

Maybe more work

Bed

This may sound depressing to you, but it's not. How do you think successful people become successful?

They follow routines.

On the morning after Bonnie's unexpected arrival, my alarm went off at six a.m. as usual. By 6:02, I'd pulled on my spandex and was striding into the kitchen, where my coffee maker had just beeped to tell me it was done. I filled my mug and looked across my immaculate kitchen for traces of Wiener's gross black fur, but didn't find any. His food and water bowls, basic copper-toned ones with no lame dog paw designs, could be considered unobtrusive accents if you were in the right headspace, I decided. As long as I never tripped over them, we were going to be fine.

With the warm mug nestled between my hands, I looked at Bonnie's closed door and felt an unexpected wave of tenderness pass over me. Was it kind of nice that my sister and I were living together again?

But a minute later, my heart was pounding out of my chest and all my sweet emotions had been replaced by the million nightmares I could see coming. The fact that Bonnie's new room was also the office was the first issue. What if I wanted to work at night? What if Wiener peed in there?

Propelled by anger about a future that hadn't happened yet—I could not get the vision of her nacho staining my spotless white interior out of my head—I had a livelier jog than usual, and by the time I got home, I had recommitted to my plan of acting like the more generous person I wanted to become. My recommitment was so devout that when I spotted Mom's breadstick still lodged on top of the hedge, I grabbed the broom from the garage and smacked it off like I was a hockey star. It flew into the street, and I sprinted after it, swiping the chunk of bread off the asphalt like I was beating an imaginary player to it. Then I slam-dunked it into the trash can. *Aah.* It was so satisfying when things got delivered to the places where they belonged—which, in my opinion, was usually within the smooth and sweaty confines of a Hefty.

I showered, then plucked the items from my closet that I'd mentally chosen while on my jog: a well-made white T-shirt and a pair of low-slung black joggers that said, *I will not burden you, Stevie. I will not implore you to fit into any specific form.*

Next, makeup. I didn't like makeup, but I was too vain to cut it out entirely. So I spent three minutes doing it. I thought that was a pretty good deal. Three dreaded minutes for a better-looking face. I slapped some tinted moisturizer onto my cheeks and forehead, dabbed heavier concealer around my eyes, curled my eyelashes, applied some Chapstick, and I was done.

I then walked into the living room, planted my hands on my waist like Wonder Woman, and mentally chanted my affirmations.

I am La Jolla's number one decluttering guru.

I am La Jolla's number one decluttering guru.

I am La Jolla's number one decluttering guru.

As I chanted, my mind wandered to other matters. So rude that Bonnie had called me Inspector Gadget. Would I need a sweater today? What was Stella doing right now?

What was Chris doing right now?

I am La Jolla's number one decluttering guru.

How had I become a woman who chanted affirmations to herself while doing this ridiculous pose?

Because it was supposed to make me feel better.

I would have done anything to feel better.

I am La Jolla's number one decluttering guru.

At seven fifteen, I still hadn't heard anything from the other side of the house, which meant that Bonnie was not showering or getting dressed or preparing to take Wiener out for a walk. Despite her fiery declaration that she wouldn't fail at this job, I was pretty sure that in forty-five minutes, she was going to fail at this job. And maybe that would be great. If she slept through work, that would be a reason to fire her.

The next part of my routine was my least-favorite part: writing for thirty minutes. Calling it a "book" was too much pressure, so I referred to it as my "project." Why was I writing this project? Because *The Life-Changing Magic of Tidying Up* had sold zillions of copies, and because all serious entrepreneurs had books these days. I mean, it was just what you did.

Without too much ceremony, and while remembering what Henrietta said—*Any words are better than no words, goddess!*—I sat down at the kitchen table with my yellow legal pad and my blue Pilot G2 roller.

I told myself not to check my phone.

Then I checked my phone.

This happened every morning.

I hit the *O* for Organizely. I was still waiting on two reviews, but I'd been waiting for a while, so I was not expecting to see that Karoline Kraz had given me five stars! I mimed a scream, with my arms cramped close to my body like a T rex, which is how my muscles react when I get overly excited. Five-star reviews were incredibly rare. This was one of only three I'd ever received.

Despite the victory, though, I was still losing to Ursula. Karoline's review hadn't been enough to bump up my average score of 4.6. And Ursula was still at 4.8. Then—dang—I noticed that she'd gotten two more reviews, bringing her total to seventy-one. How was a seventy-year-old working so fast? Was she on drugs?

These were always the questions I asked, and they were always followed by the same self-talk. Ursula's efficiency was bound to dwindle at some point—especially if she was on drugs. And even if she stayed at her current pace, I was going to dethrone her.

How exactly?

Stamina, hope, and a more detailed plan that hadn't fully materialized yet.

A marvelously rigid woman, that Stevie Green.

This was what Karoline had written about me. I assumed she'd probably meant to write marvelous *and* rigid?

Karoline was one of Mom's yoga buddies, and a serious hoarder—but only of houseplants. "Because I grew up in ze forest!" she cried in her German accent, which seemed overly patriotic given that she'd lived in La Jolla for forty years.

Plants were a sign of life and momentum, so that was great, but in Karoline's case, it was too much momentum. She'd let a vine curl its way around a sofa in one of the rooms she never used, and this vine had sprouted more vines, and now the room was basically a greenhouse. And this was only one room. In total, Karoline had 341 plants spread throughout her house. She was addicted to Plantopia and to their coupons. *Buy one get one half off!* She went several times a week and knew all the employees by name. Her car always had dirt in it. She'd stopped turning on the fans in her house, because when she did, the sound of flapping leaves was too much.

In a phrase, Karoline's plant situation was *out of control*. It also presented me with an issue I'd not yet encountered. What was the protocol for decluttering live organisms?

The solution soon became clear. Karoline had a huge yard. I suggested a planting ceremony. In the end, she said *yes, but outside* to 326 plants. Her fifteen favorites stayed in her bedroom.

The Karoline job had been ideal. She'd given me new insight into the world of indoor vegetation, five stars, and fresh fodder for my *project*.

Is it easier to part with inanimate objects than it is to part with live organisms?

In the end, I'd argued that no, the fact of one's attachment, rather than the object of one's attachment, was the problem.

If you're obsessed with plants, that's one thing. If you're obsessed with your ex's suit collection, that's another thing. But ultimately, it's all the same thing: obsession.

The suit collection reference was inspired by Dina, another of Mom's yoga friends. Dina was an example of a not-ideal client. She had given me a 3.9. Mom's response to this was "Poor baby, she's in pain." And Mom was right. Dina was in pain—hip pain, specifically. She wouldn't stop talking about it. She was also four years into the longest divorce of her life with no end in sight.

On her Freedom Day, Dina had had a semi–nervous breakdown when we got to her ex's closet. "I sort of want to keep all his suits," she said at first. After a few hours of her crying and me explaining and re-explaining the concept of "yes vs. no"—a concept which left no room for answers other than yes or no, and therefore excluded "sort of"— Dina decided that, fine, she would relinquish all but three of the suits.

This was supposed to be the end of the story, but it wasn't. A week later, Dina had regrets. She called me in a panic. Her hip pain was flaring up, and also, could we get the suits back? Well, they belonged to Goodwill now, I told her, so not really. Dina rushed to get off the phone, then sped to Goodwill to save the suits, but they were gone. Later that day, she posted her 3.9 rating and her review, in which she claimed that she'd been "brainwashed."

In my experience so far, the clients who were truly ready for a new life gave the best reviews. ("Stevie Green saved me!") And the clients who were not truly ready for a new life were the ones most likely to bring down my star count. ("Brainwashed.")

The funny thing about people is that they all say they want freedom, but most of them are lying. People don't want freedom. They want to *talk* about wanting freedom while continuing to *not* do the things that will lead them to freedom. It's like talking about wanting abs but never doing sit-ups, and this place—this never-enough place—is where most people live.

I'm not where I want to be, and I'm sad.

Complaining about not having what you want makes

you a lot of friends, because everyone else is complaining about the same thing.

I want, I want, I want.

Okay, yeah, but what are you *doing*?

Less feeling, more doing, I scribbled on the legal pad. *It's what you actually do that counts.*

Taking my own advice, I then wrote for my allotted thirty minutes—while poised at a perfect ninety-degree angle, with my elbows also falling at a perfect ninety-degree angle, because ergonomically speaking, this is the perfect way to work. My prose morphed from sentences to bullet points.

Freedom.

Self-created jail.

Never enough.

Wine sucks, don't do it.

I crossed that last line out.

"It's okay, Stevie," I said to myself. "You're fine."

When 7:59 turned to 8:00, I laid down my pen and went to knock on Bonnie's door.

No answer.

I knocked harder.

Nothing.

I sighed loudly, hoping she could hear me, and just as I was about to set my hand on the doorknob—*whoosh!*—Wiener sprinted past me like he was on fire, and then there was Bonnie, and she looked like somebody else. Or like herself, but a better version, all dressed and coiffed and beaming. Her cheeks shone like new apples, her skin was luminous, the glint in her eyes was determined as hell. She could have been an Anthropologie model in her new boho-chic outfit: light green pants and an off-white peasant shirt patterned in yellow flowers. It was all very impressive, except for the puka-shell necklace, which was still around her neck.

"Morning!" she sang.

I peered into the room. It was clean, no nachos in sight. "You folded up your bed."

"Yes, I did, boss!" Bonnie shrilled into my ear as she stepped past me to open the back door for Wiener, who was jittering like a madman on a coke bender. I thought he might hit his head on the door frame on the way out, but he didn't. After he'd buzzed outside, Bonnie turned to me and smiled so hard and for so long that her face turned red. I waited for her to stop. She kept going.

"You're going to break your jaw off."

"Ugh." She dropped the smile.

After a brief pause, during which I knew she wanted me to compliment her outfit and I silently refused, she burst into a catwalk twirl and said, "Well? What do you think? Do you *approve*?"

"Yes," I said. "Minus that necklace."

"It's vintage" was her excuse. "A wise old man gave it to me in Hawaii."

Trash, I thought, but didn't say.

"We have two clients today," I told her. "A consultation with a guy named Everett Rossbaum this afternoon. Maybe a big job. And this morning, we have a meeting with someone from our past." I hesitated. "Actually, I'm not going to tell you who it is."

"Who is it?"

I glared at her. "Dude."

She relented. "Fine."

Really, I was glad that Bonnie would be coming to Brad Rose's house with me, because every time I'd pictured going there alone, I didn't like it. I knew I probably had nothing to worry about. But still. With Bonnie, it would be easier. She could be our buffer, and she was the ideal buffer, because she knew Brad. They'd been on the surf team together.

"Let's sit at the desk, and I'll give you a quick tutorial before we have to leave."

Bonnie scrunched her face in apology first, which I appreciated. "Can I eat breakfast first? I'm dying."

I told myself to let it go and be cool and free-flowing, but I also thought it was an unacceptable request. "You realize that at a normal job, you would eat *before* work starts, right?"

Bonnie nodded deferentially—the correct response—and I made a more heartfelt attempt at being the person I wanted to be. "I guess we don't need to sit at the desk." I compromised. "We can sit in the kitchen. I can be flexible."

I can be flexible, I can be flexible.

I kept repeating this in my head as I watched Bonnie career around my kitchen. Observing her carelessness was agitating, but in another way I was inspired. It must have felt good to be Bonnie. She was a bull in a china shop, stomping around, not caring about her wreckage. I could be a bull in a china shop, too, but then later, I always found out I was also the china. Bonnie was only the bull. She spilled coffee grounds on the floor and didn't even notice.

"Are you going to clean that up?"

"It's, like, a light dusting," she muttered, yanking the dish towel off the oven bar.

As I watched her attempt to gather the grounds with the towel—not the most efficient choice—I had an instant flashback, which I told myself not to share, then did. "Remember when we were little and Mom took us to see that Tibetan mandala and you stuck your hand in it?"

"I'm going to pretend like you're not being a passive-aggressive bitch right now," Bonnie sang, flinging open the cabinet doors in search of a bowl, then squatting to inspect the fridge, which was stocked with my usual products: yogurt, tons of produce, and a bunch of different kinds of nuts and seeds in mason jars, which I liked to refrigerate because it kept them crunchy.

"Speaking of monks . . ." Bonnie segued, pulling out the yogurt and the jar of macadamia nuts. She jangled through the drawer to find my largest spoon and scooped the yogurt out ferociously, like it was snow and she was shoveling to save her life. She piled it all the way to the top, then sprinkled the entire surface with macadamia nuts until no white was showing. Somehow, she still found room to add a banana, which she didn't thinly slice with a sharp knife as I would have done, but ripped into four stumpy pieces with the dexterity of a gorilla. Last, she lathered her winter wonderland in a thick coat of honey. Too impatient to wait for the honey to drip from the spoon, she nudged it off with her finger, then stuck her finger in her mouth.

"It's amazing to me how many adults think it's okay to suck on a finger in public," I said. "Pretty much every time I go to a restaurant, there's an adult excavating behind a molar."

"I just got dumped, asshole." Bonnie slumped into the chair across from me. Her eyes fell to the legal pad. "What's that?"

"A project."

"*A project?*"

"I have a long way to go."

Bonnie gave me a contemplative stare as she tick-tocked her yogurt-streaked spoon back and forth. "Is it true you stopped drinking?"

"I'm taking a break," I said casually.

"When was the last time you got wasted?"

"It's been a while," I said, unfortunately recalling Jim or John or whatever his name was and that birthmark on his neck that was shaped like a country, but I still hadn't figured out which one.

Bonnie pondered my face some more. "Don't you think it's weird that you're taking a break now, but you didn't take one after that accident?"

"No. Why is it weird?"

"Weren't you drunk when they hit you?"

"That's not the point!"

"Jeez," Bonnie said. "I'm just trying to conversate with you."

I noticed my leg was bouncing. "'Conversate' is not a word."

"It is now. I heard about it on NPR. Anyway, you seem better."

"It's good to see you, too, sister."

Bonnie dropped her head forward, a small surrender. "Please don't be mad at me forever. I'm here now. I'm sorry I was a dick before. It was me, not you, okay?"

I complied with an "okay," although I didn't really understand how it could have been *not* about me, and then Bonnie, with that slightly damaged look in her eyes that she reserved for thinking about our dead father, said, "You look exactly like dad now that your hair's short."

Annoyingly, I knew this to be true. Mom had said the same thing several times.

"Bonnie, this is a job. I need you to pay attention."

Bonnie saluted me. "Yes, boss."

I asked her to please never salute me again as I opened the Organizely app and passed her the phone. "All we have to do is get a higher score than Ursula de Santis. That's it. One clear goal."

Bonnie's eyes lit up. "We have an enemy? You know I love a fight."

"It's not a *fight*. It's very civil."

Her eyes flicked over the screen. "We're way behind. That sucks. Why are we so far behind?"

"It doesn't matter. All we need to do now is win."

"Oh, we will," Bonnie assured me. She picked up her phone. "I'm Insta-ing Ursula's face so I can hate her visually."

"Ursula doesn't do social media."

Bonnie was startled. "How is she existing?"

"Word of mouth. She's been decluttering since the eighties."

"Old-school." Half a second later, in reaction to the picture of Ursula she'd Googled, she asked, "What is she? Like, fifty?"

"Seventy. She's married to a plastic surgeon."

Bonnie, with a spoon in one hand and her phone in the other, scooped more yogurt from her bowl with the grace of a toddler while scrolling through the images of Ursula and making comments about them. "She looks great . . . great face-lift . . . girlfriend loves a cardigan."

"We're going to kick her ass," I said.

"Oh, we're going to *pulverize* her," Bonnie echoed with force, which I had to admit was nice.

"Right, and here's how it works. The purpose of decluttering is to feel lighter in the world, right?"

Bonnie thought about that. "What if you're fat?"

"Bonnie!"

"Sorry."

I took a deep breath. Then I made up an ocean metaphor I thought would resonate with Bonnie. The metaphor might have been built for a toddler. As Bonnie continued to look at her phone—because Bonnie was never not looking at her phone—I said, "The point is to feel streamlined. Imagine a dolphin with a bunch of furniture on its back."

"Sucks."

"Exactly. The dolphin needs to get rid of the furniture. But the dolphin can't see that this is true because the dolphin is blind in some areas. So we present the dolphin with a question."

"Does this furniture spark joy?"

"No, we hate Marie Kondo," I said. "Not officially, but just between us, we hate her."

"Great," Bonnie said. "I hate her. So what's our question?"

I held out one hand. "Yes to the furniture?" And then the other. "Or no to the furniture?"

Bonnie looked up from her phone so I could see her scowl clearly. "Seriously?"

"And the dolphin has five seconds to answer."

"That's wack," Bonnie said, and before a pause even had time to become a pause, her eyes were back on her phone. "Can I give you some advice about your Instagram?"

This was the moment I realized that Bonnie could be genuinely useful to me. I showed her none of my excitement, of course. I pretended I wanted nothing from her at all when I said, "Fine."

"Well," Bonnie began, and then with great articulation—more than I thought she possessed—she laid out her feedback:

a.   the language across the board was cheesy as hell;

b.   the stock photos should all become personal photos ("Nobody cares about some random-ass soap configuration; they want the *story* behind it"); and

c.   "Don't tell people your website is coming soon. You don't need a website. People can DM you. Wake up and smell the avocado toast, home fry."

Before I could tell Bonnie that I was well aware of avocado toast, she clinked her spoon against her bowl and said,

"Wait, that's the answer! Ursula can keep the Boomers and the Gen Xers. We'll take the millennials. *That's* how we're going to win."

I didn't think it was a bad idea.

In fact, it was a good one.

"And the way to take the millennials is through Instagram," Bonnie went on, "which I'm going to revolutionize for you now. What's your password?"

I hesitated.

"I need to ask you a question first."

"Yeah?"

"I thought you'd want to hang out more when I moved back here, but you haven't. Why?"

"Sorry," Bonnie said, and she did look truly sorry.

"I don't want an apology. I want to know why."

Bonnie set her phone down. "Stevie, the last time I saw you, you were swimming in the pool with all your clothes on. At, like, noon."

I had no idea what she was talking about.

"Sorry," she said. "I don't want to embarrass you."

"No, it's okay," I said, even though of course it wasn't.

After that, I gave her the password. I was too ashamed to ask any more questions.

This was my first mistake.

CHAPTER 11

stevie

On the drive to Brad Rose's house, I checked myself out in the rearview and Bonnie said, "Who are you posing for?"

Then she held up her phone and took a picture of me.

"Stop!"

"Sorry, but you look hot."

"I forgot how annoying you are with a camera."

"Yeah, well," Bonnie said, her eyes back on her phone.

We drove on in silence.

You know when you're pretending you don't care about something and then you realize that the only reason you're pretending so hard is because you actually care a lot? Like much more than you would like to admit?

As we headed into Bird Rock, aka where Brad Rose lived, it hit me. I did care. And I was nervous.

The deal with Brad Rose:

In high school, Brad had had a crush on me for a long time, I finally gave in, we dated for a few months the summer before senior year, I slept with him three or four or seven times while very drunk, and then I called it off. Brad called me a heartbreaker and stopped speaking to me. Then I fell from grace. Then he won the election that I was supposed to have won. I hadn't seen him since graduation.

Given the friendly tone of his messages—*Can't wait to see you!*—I wasn't nervous that he was still angry with me. I was nervous because I'd decided that maybe Brad Rose would be the answer to all my life's problems.

My first goal was to beat Ursula and get my own success, because obviously a primary goal should entail only the primary person in your life, which is you. My second goal was about folding someone in. I had never had a long-term relationship, and now I wanted one.

Brad hadn't worked out in the past because we were young and I was a mess, but now it was different. Now the story had changed.

Was Brad Rose the one who got away?

This was the new story.

When he wrote to me, three things happened:

1. I almost fell over, I was so surprised.
2. I decided it might be a sign.
3. I Googled him.

What I'd learned from Google was that Brad owned a surf school and he was still hot.

Imagine David Beckham.

Brad was David Beckham.

Caught in my mind, which was where I spent most of my time caught, I'd almost forgotten that Bonnie was in the car until she said, "I can't believe Dwight is traveling through South America right now eating ayahuasca with a fucking twelve-year-old."

What I took from this was a reminder that things can change drastically and without warning. Which is either bad or good, depending on the thing.

"I'm sorry, Bonnie," I said. "And it seems so unlike Dwight. I thought he was a clock-in, clock-out type of guy."

"He was!" Bonnie said. "I still can't believe he quit his job." Then, in a meeker voice: "But he changed. And I didn't change with him. And now I can't stop looking at Yvonne's Instagram."

I summoned my boss tone, which wasn't so different from the tone of an older, wiser sister. "Bonnie, Instagram happiness is not real happiness. Please go into airplane mode. I need you on your A game."

Bonnie made a growling noise and gazed into the middle distance. "I seriously don't know who I am right now, Stevie."

"It's very unlike you to say that."

"Exactly," Bonnie said. "I'm not me right now."

I was still nervous by the time we arrived at Brad's, so I pretended not to be. What else was I supposed to do?

Brad, like Stella, lived right on the water. His house was a rustic A-frame with dark wooden shingles that probably hadn't been redone since his dad bought it in the seventies. 1972, to be exact. I'd found the deed online. I didn't know the Roses owned this house because it wasn't the house that

Brad had grown up in. Now he was the legal owner. His dad had transferred the deed to him a few years earlier.

Before we got out of the car, I reminded myself that I was not a see-through person. *If you believe in you, then he'll believe in you.* Normally, this was when I'd open the center console to count my bottles, but with Bonnie in the car, I couldn't.

"What's the goal?" I quizzed her.

"Pulverize Ursula de Santis," Bonnie said.

"Right, by getting five stars."

I thought about raising my hand for a high five, but that seemed too lame. So we just got out of the car.

Bonnie was in a heavy mood. Head down, she loped forward like there were bowling balls attached to her feet. I strode confidently. I imagined that if Chris were watching, she would have been impressed.

Bonnie had identified two long boards resting against Brad's fence and was now saying, "Wait, I know these boards."

She moved closer to inspect. Brad, since forever, had tagged his own boards with a rose. That was his thing. Upon seeing the roses, Bonnie tuned to me, her face contorted in a way that wouldn't make sense until much, much later, and just as she said, "Oh god, not Brad Rose," there was Brad Rose in real life, jogging down his steps.

"Stevie!"

My first thought: Brad looked *good*, even better in person than he had on Google. He jogged in that way that surfers and lifeguards do, with a tight, powerful bounce that seems completely effortless.

Also: that sandy blond hair, those forever-chapped lips, those eyes. They were a startling blue.

Oh, and Brad was six feet four.

He wrapped his long arms around me. "It's so good to see you!" he said.

"It's so good to see you, too."

Even in those first moments, it was clear that Brad the high school boy was now a man. There was a maturity in the way he set his big hand on the back of my head, and a sweetness, too—maybe an acknowledgment of everything we'd been through together.

When Brad let me go, the blue of his eyes startled me again, and when he smiled, with one side of his mouth pulling up before the other side, I sank into a comfortably familiar place: *Oh yeah, I remember you.*

Bonnie said his name like it was something dirty.

"Brad Rose?"

Then she stuck out her foot like fifth position in ballet class, but the bitchy version. "What. The. Fuck."

"Bonnie!"

Brad seemed very surprised to see Bonnie, and he seemed to get smaller, too, nervously scratching his elbow as he approached her like a zookeeper approaches a feral animal. Instead of diving in to hug her, he asked first. "Can I hug you?"

Bonnie looked at me. She said nothing, but her face was still saying, *What. The. Fuck.*

I held up my palm and mouthed, *Five*, as in five stars.

Bonnie twisted her mouth into the fakest smile, the same one she'd presented me with that morning that I told her was going to break her jaw off. In the voice of an over-caffeinated telemarketer, she exclaimed, "It's *great* to see you, Brad!"

I had no idea what was going on between Bonnie and Brad, but if I'd had to guess, it would have been either that (a) there was no actual reason; Brad was just one of the many people Bonnie disliked; or (b) Bonnie was still angry on my behalf that Brad had beat me in the election in high school. Since both options ended in the same place—Bonnie's anger—and since she was angry about a lot of things, and a firecracker of a person in general, I already knew, even before she'd explained her stance, that I wouldn't be taking her feelings about Brad very seriously.

To Bonnie's credit, she managed to bag her feelings and be polite throughout the consultation—or polite with an edge, which was her way. There was an upside, though, to Bonnie's bluntness. She asked the questions I wanted answers to but didn't have the gall to ask myself.

Upon entering his basically vacant abode, she said, "Um, Brad? Why do you need a decluttering? There's nothing in here." She swept her hand over the stripped-down landscape of the living room, which included one couch, one chair, one coffee table, and one yellowed surfing poster that was affixed to the wall with mismatched thumbtacks and curling at the edges. Then she spun around and jokingly asked a serious question.

"Was it just so you could see Stevie again?"

Brad folded his arms across his chest. "What?"

Instead of directly answering the question, Brad explained why he had contacted me when he did. "My buddy works over at Plantopia, and that German chick Karoline told him about you and he mentioned you to me, and I was like, *Holy crap, I should write to Stevie!*" He then went on to tell us about why he needed help. It was because he had a collection problem. "I guess I'd call them trinkets? From Bali, Thailand, Australia, whatever. They're crowding my style."

I tuned out of the conversation to zone in on Brad's enormous biceps and the enormity of him in general and how in his presence, I just felt . . . safe. When I tuned back in, Brad was saying, "Like seven didgeridoos. Here, I'll show you."

And then we were following him down the stairs to a second living room filled with furniture that was identical to the furniture in the upstairs living room, but with a pool table instead of a coffee table. Bonnie's reaction to this was the same as mine, only she said it aloud. "Bachelor pad."

Brad took the feedback well. "Ha, I guess you're right. I should probs get rid of the pool table."

And the graphic tee you're wearing and your Vans slip-ons and definitely the word "probs," I thought but did not say. The more important point here was that Brad seemed open to change. He *wanted* change. Which meant that I could mold him.

"You should *absolutely* get rid of the pool table," Bonnie said to Brad.

"I have a method that makes these choices super easy," I said. "I'll explain it after the tour."

"Cool," Brad said. "The tour's almost over. Small house."

There were two doors downstairs, both closed. Brad opened the first one. "This is my bedroom."

White bedding. A blue accent wall. The room looked like a wave. How fitting. What struck me most poignantly was the mason jar half-full of water on Brad's bedside table. It just seemed so intimate. Brad Rose drank water from this mason jar in bed.

He motioned toward the haphazard closet. "I actually might need help getting rid of some old, fug clothes," he said. "But the bigger problem is in here."

I added "fug" to my list of things to change about Brad, and he opened the second door, revealing possibly hundreds of dusty wooden objects. A lot of them looked tribal. Some were painted vibrant colors.

Bonnie snapped a pic. "For Instagram," she explained to Brad, who said, "Obvs."

We moved back upstairs to "Living Room One," as Bonnie called it with a smirk, and I explained how the process worked. Bonnie sat in the lone chair and Brad sat next to me on the couch and every time I said something he found appealing, he touched my knee or my arm and said "Yeah!" or "Totes!"

I liked the attention. I liked his eyes. I liked his voice. And I really liked his smell, which was like coconut sunscreen and pine needles, embedded in a salty mist.

I was veering toward the end of my spiel. "So with every item, you'll ask"—cue right hand—"yes"—cue left hand—"or no?"

Brad smiled. "Rad," he said, as the waves crashed poetically behind him.

"It's like a dolphin," Bonnie explained. "You want to be streamlined. And not carrying an old pool table on your back." She flashed a one-second jawbreaker grimace at Brad. "You know?"

Brad laughed. "Got it." Then he asked my sister thoughtful questions. "How've you been, Bonnie? You still surfing?"

Bonnie sighed, then said in her telemarketer voice, "Yes, Brad, I am."

"Awesome."

Bonnie continued her pattern of acting like an asshole and then guiltily making up for it when she managed to ask Brad one thoughtful question in return.

"How's your surf school going?"

Pretending that you haven't Googled somebody even though you have is the worst type of lying, but I went for it anyway.

"You run a surf school?" I asked genuinely enough. But then I sort of overdid it. "That's so cool. Like, that's seriously so cool."

In response to my gushing, I could feel Bonnie's *What. The. Fuck.* stare boring a hole into the side of my face as Brad told us his surf school was going super well. It had just celebrated its ten-year anniversary, and the best part about it was seeing how getting out in nature had the power to get some teenagers out of their depression. We all agreed that the teenage years were the absolute worst, but nobody mentioned the specifics of our shared past. We all looked at our feet for a brief awkward moment, and then we filled the silence with more updates about what we'd been doing since high school.

I recounted the last twenty years of my life with a positive spin. What other option did I have? I changed "bartending gigs" to "fun random gigs" and minimized the fourteen cities I'd lived in to a cool "bunch," promptly ending on the high note of my finding my true calling, decluttering. I told the story of how it had evolved, happy with how organic it was. "And then, after I finished helping my mom move out of her old house, she said, 'You should start a business.' So I did. And now I'm just back here in La Jolla jogging at the Shores every morning like a real native and seeing clients and, yeah, I mean it feels very full circle."

Brad said that was amazing. "Full circles are the best." Then he asked Bonnie what she'd been up to besides surfing.

Bonnie kept it short. "Getting dumped."

"Oh man, that blows," Brad said. "I'm so sorry. I just broke up with someone, too. It's the worst."

"When?" Bonnie asked.

"Like two weeks ago?"

"So this *just* happened," Bonnie said, uncrossing her legs and setting her elbows on her knees like a sports coach. "And then you wrote to Stevie?"

Brad shrugged. "Serendipity."

"Right," Bonnie said, unconvinced. Then she checked her phone. "It's been an hour. We should go. Consultations are an hour, right, Stevie?"

"Right. Brad, let's set a date for your Freedom Day."

"The sooner the better," Brad said, pulling his phone out of his board shorts. "Sunday?"

"Sure," I said. "I could squeeze you in in the morning?"

"Can't wait," Brad said.

"Me neither," Bonnie said dryly.

And then we followed Brad to the door. Physically, he

was perfect. On paper, he was perfect. A few cosmetic elements would need to change, but my overwhelming feeling at the end of the consultation was this: *I am now 90 percent sure that Brad Rose is the one.*

Out in the driveway, he hugged me again with genuine affection, and then he and Bonnie patted each other's backs like bros.

"Have you seen anyone else from high school since you've been back, Stevie?"

"No," I said. "Well, except for Chris Dane. We ran into each other randomly."

I don't know why I told them this, because I wasn't ready to talk about her yet, and I wasn't ready for their reactions either.

"Chris Dane?" Bonnie stopped moving. *"Really?"*

A melancholy blankness spread over Brad's chiseled face. I recognized this look from the day I dumped him, and I remembered the thing he'd said, too.

It's Chris, isn't it?

CHAPTER 12

stevie

The second we'd pulled out of Brad's driveway, Bonnie said, "He's obsessed with you, Stevie, and he has been forever. It's creepy."

"Maybe I *want* someone to be obsessed with me right now."

Bonnie swiveled to face me like a robot at half speed. "Oh my god," she said. "Are you thinking of boning Brad Rose?"

"Why do you hate him so much?" I asked her. "Are you mad he won that stupid election?"

"No," Bonnie said. "Also, who cares? That was so long ago."

"You know Chris did it, right?"

"I—"

"Or who do you do think did it?"

"I think whatever you think," Bonnie said, absentmindedly pulling at the latch on the center console.

"Stop that," I said, pushing her hand away.

"Please turn right at the next light for tacos," Bonnie said.

"You have no opinion about who did it? You think whatever I think? That's very unlike you, Bonnie."

"I told you, I'm not me right now!" Bonnie let her head fall back and groaned. "I can't believe you saw Chris. What happened? I want a play-by-play."

"It was . . . not great," I said, remembering the shape of Chris's mouth, and then unfortunately remembering what that mouth had told me: *It was painful to watch.* "She still won't admit to her crime. Which seems weird since she's a therapist. Aren't therapists supposed to be all about honesty?"

"And she's sober," Bonnie said, "and those people are all about honesty, too."

I knew Chris was sober because my mom wouldn't shut up about it. *Chris is sober! She goes to those meetings! Maybe you should go to those meetings?*

"Exactly," I said. "It's weird. Why not just confess?"

"Totally," Bonnie agreed, and then, as if she'd been suddenly electrocuted, she screamed, "Turn right for tacos!"

"I *am* turning right!"

She sat back in her seat then, hopefully ashamed of her behavior, and murmured, "Thank you."

I made the right, using both hands to turn the wheel, and that's when Bonnie opened the center console, and before I could do anything about it, she whipped out one of the bottles I'd stashed there. It wasn't even a nice brand.

"Sutter Home?" She turned. "I thought you stopped drinking."

I snatched the bottle, dropped it back in with the others, and smacked the console shut. "I keep them close by to remind me not to drink."

Bonnie left a brutal pause here. "Do you realize how crazy that sounds?"

Of course I knew it *sounded* crazy, but that didn't mean it *was* crazy. There was a difference. "Bonnie, please stay out of my business."

Bonnie tapped the center console. "I'm going to fill those with water when you're not looking."

"Don't!"

"Why do you care if you're not going to drink them?"

I didn't answer. I drove down the sunny street, trying to breathe evenly, remembering how far I'd come and why. I'd gone six months without drinking, and maybe it was only *because* I'd kept those mini bottles around. Without them, I might have forgotten how bad it had gotten. I thought of John or Jim or whatever his name was, and the country-shaped birthmark on his neck, which I now thought might have been an island, not a country. Crete? Madagascar? Why was I still trying to figure it out?

Bonnie had gone on talking. *Blah blah blah, worried about you. Blah blah blah, playing with fire. Blah blah blah, the accident.*

"Stop bringing up the accident, Bonnie."

"You almost *died.*"

"Okay, but I didn't die, so it's not a big deal."

"Mom said you have a fat scar on your back. Is that true?"

I laughed. "Yes, but because it's on my back I conveniently never have to see it unless I want to."

"Why are you laughing?" Bonnie said. "It's not funny."

I stopped laughing and changed the subject. Or I returned the subject back to Brad, because I'd just decided that every time John/Jim popped into my head, I'd replace the thoughts of him with ones of Brad. That seemed like a smart fix.

"Seriously, tell me why you hate Brad," I said, because even though I didn't trust Bonnie's opinion, I still wanted to know what it was.

"If you end up like Dad, Stevie, I'm never going to forgive you."

I placed a gentle hand on my sister's shoulder. "Bonnie, thank you for your concern. Now can you please tell me what your deal with Brad is? I'd really like to know."

Bonnie sighed. "I think his obsession with you is, I don't know, kind of sinister? But you know what? Maybe I'm wrong. Everyone was obsessed with you in high school. You were so nice to everybody." Bonnie hesitated. "Well, except for me."

I tensed. "I wasn't *that* mean to you, was I?"

"Stevie," Bonnie said.

At this point in my life, my recollection of high school had been so overshadowed by the inciting incident that the rest of it had become a blur, and that made sense. I was either hyperfocused on schoolwork or sleeping or drunk the whole time.

"How was I mean to you?" I asked her. I didn't want to know, but of course I also did.

Bonnie, with no hesitation, started counting the ways. "You told me you were the prettier one. You made me go to

your drug dealer's house with you in the middle of the night.
You took me to Sephora when my arm was broken and stuck
a bunch of Stila eyeliners in my cast so that if we got caught,
I'd go down, not you."

"But we didn't get caught," I said.

"No, you never got caught for anything."

I finished the thought for her. "Until I did."

CHAPTER 13

stevie

We ate tacos and debriefed Mom by the pool.

"Brad—"

"Lives in a house with nothing in it," Bonnie said.

"He has a collection problem."

"Trinkets. Which are fug."

"He did use the word 'fug,'" I said, "but not about the trinkets."

"What is 'fug'?" Mom asked.

"Short for fugly."

"Fucking ugly," Bonnie said. "And he has two living rooms."

"And nice bedding."

"Was it nice?" Bonnie said. "I thought it was basic."

"I thought it was nice."

"And Stevie wants to sleep with him," Bonnie said. "That's the lede we're burying."

"And Bonnie won't tell me why she hates him," I said to

Mom, who was feeding Wiener a piece of chicken from her taco.

Mom didn't ask Bonnie why she hated Brad. She asked me if I really wanted to sleep with him. "Do you, Stevie?"

"I don't know. Maybe. Why is that a big deal?"

Mom smiled at me with a suspicious amount of kindness in her eyes. She didn't literally shrug, but she had the aura of a person who might have been shrugging inside. "No reason," she said. "Just wondering."

Bonnie took a too-big bite of her taco. She'd ordered seven of them. Because *it's a lucky number, asshole*, she'd told me. With her mouth full and her head tipped back so the food wouldn't fall out, she said, "And Stevie and Chris Dane are friends again and she won't talk about it."

"We're not *friends*. We ran into each other at the Pannikin."

"I know," Mom said. "She called me right afterward."

"What did she say?" I asked.

"She said your hair looks fabulous."

I felt my face flush, which annoyed me. I didn't want to care about what Chris thought of me. I wanted to stay angry. "Yeah?" I said. "What else?"

Mom rolled her shoulders back. "She might have been somewhat upset that you're still upset."

"About her *ruining* my life," I finished.

"I don't think Chris made those flyers, Stevie," Mom said.

"How would you know?"

"Chris Dane is one of the most wonderful people I've ever met."

"So who do you think did it, then?"

"I have no idea, but I'm *positive* that it wasn't Chris."

"Oh my god, can we please drop this?" Bonnie said. "It's so dumb."

"Anyway, I do hope you call her," Mom said. "She's expecting your call."

Again, the face flush. The prickly armpits. The flutter of happiness. Chris Dane still cared about me.

And so I played up the opposite. As if annoyed, I said, "Great, well, you can tell her that I am expecting her apology. And I don't want to talk about this anymore. The only thing I care about is becoming number one on Organizely."

"Ursula is going *down*," Bonnie said as she unwrapped another taco.

"She needs to go down faster," Mom said.

"We *know*, Mom," Bonnie said, then went on to explain the Instagram plan that would "take the millennials."

When she was done, Mom said, "If the brand must be streamlined, as Bonnie is saying, then how does it make sense that the company is called Stevie Cleans? If it's the two of you now, then the name needs to change."

Bonnie admitted that she'd been thinking the same thing, but had been too scared to bring it up. "I thought you might get mad, Stevie." If this admission was a manipulative move on her part, then it worked. Not wanting to be scary, I allowed myself to be steamrolled.

A brainstorming session began, and one minute later we'd whittled it down to two options: Clean Green Sisters or Clean Green Decluttering Machines. The first was classic. The second was funnier, but lacked the sister element. I chose the classic, of course—I didn't want to risk being funny in the wrong way—and told myself that if Bonnie ditched me later, which she more than likely would, I could keep the name and tell everyone she was on vacation. Or whatever. Even though it seemed like a commitment, it didn't have to be forever.

"Clean Green Sisters," Bonnie narrated as she typed it in.

After several excited moments of repeating our new name with different intonations—*Clean* Green Sisters, Clean Green *Sisters*—Bonnie revealed what she'd forgotten to tell me.

"While I was inside ordering tacos, I posted the pic I took at Brad's on both of our pages and told my peeps to follow you."

I leaned over her shoulder, concerned, which turned out to be the correct way to feel. Brad's wooden trinkets looked like the bowels of an abandoned antique store. I understood that people might want to see the *Before*, but without an *After*, how was this a message about renewal?

Next I read the caption, in which Bonnie had described the *bonanza of Balinese furniture* and our *soon-to-be Ford factory ferociousness*. It ended with *Just two #noblebitches on a mission.*

"Noble bitches?"

"I think it's great," Mom said. "Very conversational."

I felt like the two of them were taking over my life, but it was also hard to argue. The post had gotten over five hundred likes on Bonnie's page, and ninety-eight likes on the company page, which we were now referring to as *our* page, although by "we," I meant everyone but me. Stubbornly, I was calling it *the* page.

"Brand voices used to be cold, but now they should sound like your friend," Bonnie explained.

"That's how I feel every time I call Amazon," Mom said. "Like I'm talking to a friend. I don't know if I like it or not."

"You do," Bonnie told her.

Mom then performed one of her signature moves, a pirouette with words. She asked a question and then answered it herself.

Question: "You need some new company pics of the both of you, do you not?"

Answer: "I'll take them."

Hopeful that this plan would lead to more visibility and therefore more clients than my original plan to do everything myself—which hadn't really been working—I succumbed to the hour-long photo shoot without argument. It turned out to be fun. Actually, it turned out to be so unexpectedly fun that I felt like I was doing something wrong.

With Mom as our leader, we went through the house, posing naturally while pretending to declutter. In the kitchen, I poured Wiener's dog food from its ugly crinkled bag into a mason jar while Bonnie sat cross-legged on the floor, holding him up like a baby, his front two paws propped in her hands. In the bathroom, I folded towels while Bonnie gave the camera a thumbs-up. In the living room, I pretended to be explaining something about organizing to Bonnie, my arm stretched long, my finger pointing at the wall.

Mom gave spirited directives.

"More! Not believable! Lift your chin! Be more real!"

She said that to me more times than she said it to Bonnie.

"Be more real!"

After hitting every room in my house, we moved on to Mom's, where she showed us her new dolls, including the just-finished redhead that she'd wrapped in a purple pleather unitard. Bonnie thought it was her. It wasn't.

"You're not the only redhead in town, Bon."

Along with the not-Bonnie doll, there were five others seated on Mom's couch. The lineup included a mermaid, a merman, and three fairies. Mom twirled her silver ponytail and said, "I'm going to ask Donna to sell the mermaid and the merman as a couple. I think they belong together, don't you?"

Bonnie looked up from her phone. *"Belong together?"*

I was just as surprised. "Are you ready to start dating, Mom?"

"Because you've never sold your dolls as a couple before," Bonnie said.

"They'll sell better as a pair, that's all," Mom said evenly, and her expression was a placid lake, same as always.

"Maybe your brand's changing," Bonnie said.

"Am I a brand?" Mom asked. "I thought I was an artist."

"We're all brands now," Bonnie said.

On the wall where most people would have installed a TV, Mom had done the same thing she'd done at Moonridge and drawn a TV instead, an ancient one with boxy buttons and an antenna, its screen blank.

"Let's get a shot of you two in front of the TV," Mom suggested, and Bonnie and I complied, sitting cross-legged and side by side and doing what we'd done as kids, which was make up stories about what could have been on the screen. "Donkey porn," Bonnie whispered. I pushed her.

"Gross." Mom, who was walking around us, snapping shots from all angles, said, "Bonnie, lift your chin. And Stevie, keep smiling, that's good, you look real."

Then Mom turned on some music and we continued the shoot out by the pool, pretending to declutter Bonnie's dump site. With the marine layer burned off and the sun pouring over the afternoon and Pat Benatar's voice (*Fire awaaaay!*) pulsing through the air, it felt like we were the stars of our very own toothpaste commercial. Not even the presence of Wiener, who was trying to climb up my shins, disturbed me. I simply ignored him.

After the shoot, we sat at the table and went through the photos together. Mom thought we looked very professional. And beautiful. And that anyone with half a brain would hire us over Ursula.

"And you look just like Dad in this one, Stevie. The way your foot's pointed out? He used to do that." Mom smiled sadly. "Thank god you stopped drinking."

Bonnie, who'd been petting Wiener's head, paused. "Sutter Home."

"What?" Mom asked.

While glaring at Bonnie, I said, "Nothing, Mom."

"You're not going to start drinking again, are you, Stevie?" Bonnie asked.

"Of course not!"

What was the difference between a truth you could feel and a truth you *thought* you could feel?

Was there a difference?

CHAPTER 14

stevie

If Everett Rossbaum's house were a hipster brand of lipstick, it would have been called Single Man's Junkyard.

An average man of average height and average looks, he opened the door wearing grease-stained sweatpants and a too-small white V-neck shirt that came from one of those three-packs you get at CVS. He had the soured, dingy aura of a person who frequently went bowling, although, as it would turn out, bowling was not his thing. Gaming was.

Everett invited us to sit on his couch, which was actually three couches pressed together in the shape of a U. The configuration faced an enormous TV screen, below which cords of various colors and lengths pooled on the unvacuumed carpet like harried, futuristic nests. Along the wall were piles of video games, stacked askew.

Everett presented us with tap water in Solo cups, and Bonnie said, "I feel like I'm at a kegger," then sank into his couch like she came over here all the time.

Everett laughed in one syllable. "Ha."

"So," Bonnie said, "who are you?"

Everett seemed at first unsure about how to explain who he was. Then he settled on this: "I'm an orthodontist and I'm Jewish."

I smiled politely in response to Everett's self-identifying statement, then began the spiel.

"Our process is simple," I began, setting my cup down between the hodgepodge of remote controls and gaming magazines on Everett's coffee table. This was my silent refusal to drink tap water. Also, I needed both hands to do the yes-or-no thing. "For each item, there are two questions." Right palm up. "Yes." Left palm up. "Or no."

Everett waited a long time, then said, "What?"

"Don't worry, I didn't get it at first either," Bonnie reassured him, then gave him some extra reassurance with a wink. "It's one of those things that's so dumb it's smart again."

"Okay," Everett said, stroking his five-o'clock shadow.

When we got around to the goals section, Everett identified his as follows: "I want a girlfriend." He traced a bushy eyebrow with his thumb, smiling sheepishly, revealing teeth that were mostly straight, and yellower than I would have expected from someone in the dental profession. "I need this place to be clean so I can bring a nice lady here."

Bonnie slapped Everett's thigh and scream-repeated his words. "A nice lady!" I couldn't tell if she was making fun of him or flirting. Either way, she was being unprofessional.

A few minutes later, when Everett got up to explain the logic behind his game piling—"because I like *Mario Kart* better than *Mario Tennis*"—I pinched Bonnie's arm and mouthed, *Sit up!* She did what I asked and retained her good posture for the rest of the hour, but this didn't fix the problem. She continued to be unprofessional while sitting up straight. Everett, though, seemed to like Bonnie's style. His face lit up every time he looked at her.

During the tour, Everett opened the door to the guest room, and two things happened.

One, Bonnie screamed.

Two, I almost passed out. The stench was health-code-violation rank. It was biohazard rank. Imagine the sourness of body odor. Now imagine it sprinkled with mold and nutritional yeast. That's what it smelled like.

We covered our faces, then resorted to mouth breathing only as we took in the mounds and mounds of dirty laundry. It was heaped on the bed. It was piled on the floor. It was like that children's book in which spaghetti takes over a town, but instead of spaghetti, it was clothes.

Bonnie took a quick picture, then said, "Close the door close the door close the door."

Everett, alarmed by our alarm, did, then set his hand on his chest. But it was more like a paw than a hand. Because Everett, I realized then, was more like a koala bear than a person.

"*Why* is this room full of dirty laundry?" I asked him.

"Doing laundry makes me anxious?"

Bonnie, sensing there might be more to it than a mere dislike of the backbreaking task of loading and unloading, gently asked Everett to say some more about that.

And that's when he revealed that until a few years ago, his mom, who lived down the street, had been doing his laundry, and after that, Dagmar had taken over, and then all laundry-doing had ceased when Dagmar had gone back to Croatia. Dagmar was Everett's ex.

"Oh, thank god, a breakup story," Bonnie said. "This is all I want to hear right now. Tell us everything."

Everett's abridged story of the relationship sounded like a poem. "We met on the Internet. We were going to get married on a sailboat. She wanted to feed me fruit every morning for the rest of my life. The first morning she fed me an apple. There was no more fruit after that. Weeks passed. Then she left."

Bonnie was rapt. "And then what?"

And then, instead of washing his dirty clothes, Everett started buying new ones from J.Crew, Dagmar's favorite American store. He also started gaming. His mom had left his first game on the porch with a note: *Do something enjoyable.*

"Is it enjoyable?" I asked.

Everett considered that. "When I'm stoned."

"But then at four a.m., you hate yourself," Bonnie said, as if she'd been struggling with a gaming addiction all her life.

Everett touched his koala bear heart as if to say, *Yes.*

I made a hard turn back to practical matters. "Please buy trash bags before Freedom Day," I instructed. "Preferably scented, double-reinforced Heftys."

Then Bonnie asked Everett more questions about his personal life, and he broke down sobbing—the uncontrollable sobs of a koala bear baby—and told us that gaming had turned him into a man he didn't want to be.

I could have told him that I knew exactly how it feels to wake up one day and realize you've wandered deep into a forest and now you are lost and have no idea how to get back to civilization, but I offered some general wisdom instead.

"Decluttering is about making space to find out who you really are and what you really want, and once you get clear on those things, you'll come to love yourself, and then you will attract love."

I delivered this information like it was a scientific fact, because I'd just read it in a book, although later I would remember that it hadn't been a book, but rather a quote stitched on a pillow on Instagram. *Love yourself and you will attract love.*

"You're going to find the perfect person at the perfect time," Bonnie promised him. "But these video games are skewing your expectations, bro. If all their female characters look like Lara Croft, then that's not real life. Real life is ugly. Which you should know! Aren't you looking into people's mouths all day?"

Everett laughed—"ha"—then blew his nose with a free paper napkin from Domino's that he'd just unleashed from his pocket.

"Domino's?" Bonnie said. "You can do better, dude."

We landed back on the U-couch to set a date for Freedom Day. Would Saturday work? Yes, Everett said, it would, and he swore to us that he wouldn't game until then. Bonnie slapped Everett's back. "Whatever you decide to do, Everett, do it with gusto." Everett nodded like this was an order and he was a soldier. Then Bonnie made us take a selfie. Then we said all the things—*so nice to meet you, see you soon, yay, we're so excited, too!*—and I wondered how much room pleasantries took up in my life.

Way too much room was my answer.

Once we were back in the car, Bonnie looked at Everett's house, which was painted sea-foam green and surrounded by a sea-foam-green picket fence—it all looked like mouthwash—and said, "You'd never guess how much he's suffering just by looking at his house, right? So many people are crying alone in their boxes, man. I feel *inspired*. And I forgot that having a job is such a good distraction. I only thought about Dwight and Yvonne having sex, like, two times while we were in there."

"I've given you a purpose in life," I said. "At least temporarily. You're welcome."

"Is this your purpose in life?" Bonnie asked. "Decluttering?"

"And becoming number one on Organizely."

"Okay, but isn't that kind of . . . arbitrary?"

"No, it's a measure of success. It's being the best. It's being the *winner*."

Bonnie stared at me. "This is about high school, isn't it? Like, this is your redo."

I was embarrassed—the embarrassment of being truly seen—but I didn't argue.

"Yes," I said, "this is my redo."

CHAPTER 15

stevie

CHRIS DANE, MFT

Her business card was embossed. I ran my thumb over her name.

Chris Dane was expecting my call. Chris Dane cared about me.

But Chris Dane had ruined my life. Chris Dane was a bad person.

But Chris Dane didn't seem like a bad person?

We'd skipped family dinner that night. Mom had gone out to dinner with Donna to discuss her dolls. Bonnie had holed up with Wiener and Netflix, and I was lying in bed wondering about the future.

I definitely wasn't going to text Chris. Because what would I say?

Let's talk.

No.

I never want to see you again.

No.

So annoying that you're friends with my mother.

But I didn't find it annoying, actually. I was glad when they became friends after running into each other at the farmer's market about a year earlier. It allowed me to keep tabs on Chris Dane from afar.

You know when you have an idea that's obviously a bad idea so you decide you absolutely won't act on it, but then a few minutes later, you come to the conclusion that you only live once, so who cares?

This was like that.

Let's talk.

Send.

CHAPTER 16

chris

SARAH, 42, DOCTOR

I checked Sarah's profile picture, then looked across the crowded restaurant for blond heads. I found a few, but the faces didn't match Sarah's. Sarah's face was strawberry-shaped. Her eyes were dark brown, and so were her eyebrows, which meant her blond hair was a dye job. This unnatural choice wouldn't have been my personal choice, but you can't have everything, can you?

This was what I often found myself saying while scrolling through Hinge.

You can't have everything, can you?

Stevie Green, though, might have had everything. Well, minus the glaring detail that she very possibly considered herself to be straight.

I checked for blond heads again. I checked the time. Where the hell was Dr. Sarah?

And then I got a text.

Let's talk.

It was from a number I didn't recognize.

Who is this?

Stevie.

Elated. That's how I felt. Because Stevie was a dear old friend. *You cannot date any more women who are confused about their sexuality, Chris*, I reminded myself. *Confused women are a deal breaker.*

Dinner tomorrow? Spice & Rice?

Yes, Stevie wrote back, and when Dr. Sarah sat down across from me and said, "Sorry I'm late," all I could think when I looked at her face was, *You look nothing like Stevie.*

CHAPTER 17

bonnie

I had a come-to-Jesus moment while watching *In Her Shoes* that night. In case you've never seen it, it's a movie about estranged sisters who don't have the same story about the past. That's super reductive, but whatever, it's all you need to know.

I cried while watching this movie. Because Toni Collette and Cameron Diaz's characters love each other so much, but they spend an hour and fifteen minutes not understanding each other and being disappointed and angry and hurt, and then in the last fifteen minutes they're like, *I love you so much!* It's a horribly uneven ratio.

My come-to-Jesus-moment was this: if Stevie and I were going to get to the love part, like the real love part that could only be attained through total honesty, then I would need to tell her about what had happened in high school.

The problem was that I couldn't.

I just couldn't.

So I devoted the rest of my night to assuaging my guilt

instead. I DM'd potential clients. I posted three new pictures. Clean Green Sisters now had over a thousand followers. This was very good. It meant that I was worth something. And it led me to form a new plan.

I would help Stevie become number one on Organizely and then would I tell her the truth. If I could prove to her that I was valuable, then maybe she wouldn't discard me?

CHAPTER 18

kit

I wasn't at dinner with Donna.

I'd stopped by the gallery to drop off the new dolls, and now I was at El Ranchero, eating flautas with a man named Douglas. It was my first-ever Internet date. Or app date. Chris had convinced me to sign up for Hinge, and I didn't tell the girls about it, because what was I? An open book?

A person should be allowed to have some secrets.

That wasn't the real reason, though. The real reason was that I didn't want them to get too excited, and I didn't want to field their questions about Douglas either.

Douglas.

Douglas's curly salt-and-pepper hair was probably why I'd chosen him. Jack's hair had been curly. I was really trying not to compare Douglas to Jack, but it was hard. Moving on was hard. Why was moving on so hard? It had been thirty-four years. I should have been healed. I should have married someone else immediately, and now maybe it was too late.

Douglas was talking about his job. "The students aren't

what they used to be," he was saying. "Much less engaged. Always on their phones." Douglas was a physics professor at UCSD, and I thought he had a chip on his shoulder. This is what happened when you got old. You acquired chips on your shoulders.

I rolled my own shoulders back and echoed the lament about phone usage. "Such a pity. But it comes in handy, too. My daughter is obsessed with her phone. She's Insta-famous. Which is apparently what you call someone who's famous on Instagram."

"You have a daughter," Douglas said.

"Two. Stevie and Bonnie. We named them after Stevie Nicks and Bonnie Raitt."

"What are they like, besides being Insta-famous?" Douglas asked, and thoughtfully sipped his margarita.

"Stevie is . . . well, she's struggled. She's incredibly bright. But very guarded. She hasn't made the best choices for herself. It's been . . . difficult. She was in a horrible accident earlier this year. But! She's doing *much* better now, thankfully. I convinced her to come back home and I'm sort of . . . nursing her back to health, I guess you could say. And Bonnie is hilarious. Very sensitive. A surfer. She has the cutest little dachshund. I always thought she'd have a job working with animals, but my girls actually just went into business together! They're both living with me again. It's funny how life works out, isn't it?"

"They *live* with you? How old are they?"

"Midthirties?"

Douglas braided his fingers together on the table. It was a professorial move. "I'm just going to be honest with you,

Kit. I don't think I can date a woman whose children still live with her. And I don't want to waste your time."

"Oh."

And then Douglas was motioning for the bill. "I'm sorry."

"I assume you don't have children?" I asked.

"No."

The waiter arrived at the table. "I'd like to pay," Douglas said, handing over his credit card, which the waiter swiped right there. He signed the bill, apologized again, and then he left.

I sat there for a while, eating the rest of the guacamole, talking myself through what had just happened. Douglas had his needs. I didn't fit into his needs. He probably didn't fit into my needs either. But what were my needs? It had been so long that I wasn't sure anymore.

The waiter came back. "Can I get you anything else?"

"Another margarita, please."

I was looking at my phone, thinking about what Douglas had said. *Always on their phones.* And then what I had said. *Such a pity.*

Without thinking about it too much, I downloaded the Instagram app and created an account.

Oh, good, "Kit Green" was available.

CHAPTER 19

stevie

Want to know what I fell asleep thinking about?

The inciting incident.

I think it's time to tell you what happened.

Ugh.

It was an ordinary day.

Isn't this always when disaster strikes? On ordinary days?

Anyway, on this ordinary day, I arrived at school early as usual. I parked in the spot closest to the entrance, and just this—me arriving early to get that prime spot—was evidence of what a good kid I was, or at least of what a good kid I appeared to be.

I was homecoming queen. I was on the honor roll. I drove a cool Jeep. My long hair was always straight-ironed. I tucked my blouses into my jeans because a tuck-in gave the impression that I was wise beyond my years, a fully formed adult who just happened to be facing the technicality of high school. I was overcompensating, sure, but that's what a façade is: an overcompensation, and a deliberate one. My physical appearance said half of what I needed to say without my speaking, and my scholastic achievements said the rest. It's amazing how much you can get away with when people trust your presentation. Wear a good blouse, tell them what they want to hear, act the part. I thought it was easy—and it *was* easy—but I'd grown cocky, and kind of lazy, too, not checking my angles carefully enough to make sure no one was looking, not doing the extra-credit assignments because I already had an A, so who cared.

I leaned over the passenger's seat of my Jeep to do a bump of coke, which had become my new normal that fall. Just a little pick-me-up. This is what I said to myself every time I snorted up that snowy power, and afterward I always thought, *Just a little pick-me-up? Sounds like a commercial for Burger King or something.*

Anyway, these are minor details. The major detail is that I'd started doing coke that summer and I couldn't stop, but because I was still performing at top level, it was fine.

So, *Just a little pick-me-up. Sounds like a commercial for Burger King or something.* I swallowed the chemical numbness at the back of my throat, then looked up at the poster tied to the fence.

STEVIE GREEN FOR PRESIDENT.

All the letters were perfectly drawn because I'd drawn them perfectly, and that was why it was supposed to be a clear win: because I was basically perfect, and also very popular. On top of looking the part and getting good grades, I was also nice to everybody.

Was this because I was a nice person?

Or was it because I wanted to be popular?

Did it matter?

I took a few gulps of water and grabbed my messenger bag, which I carried instead of a backpack because it made me seem important and serious, and then I waltzed through the beige archway of La Jolla High like I owned the world. Soon I'd be at Stanford, which had many beige archways, and they were grander and had lion statues on the sides. I just had to win the presidency, skate through the rest of senior year, and then I'd be in Palo Alto—the end.

There were a bunch of flyers on the ground. When did I notice this? I mean, I saw paper, and a lot of it, but I didn't look too closely. I was busy owning the world. If I assumed anything, it was that the flyers were for somebody's stupid band.

But then it was a lot of paper. Too much paper. The ground was almost white with paper, and it didn't stop once I'd waltzed through the archway. The flyers covered the entire campus like a blanket. Whoever had done this was very determined, and that determination inspired me to look closer.

So I picked one up.

I can't remember what I saw first.

Was it the rolled-up twenty held between my fingers like a cigarette?

Or was it Chris and I, midkiss?

Maybe I saw it all at the same time—and it hit me like an early death.

I know that because I stopped breathing.

"Oh, dang, it's that president chick," some dude standing by the science building said to his friend.

"Hot," the friend said.

Before they could see me, I flew out of there. As nonchalantly as possible, of course, even though I was on the verge of a panic attack. My feet were walking, then jogging back to the car, my head was down, and my hair was flying around my face, or floating underwater, because it felt like time had slowed. My hand fumbled with the keys. It didn't feel like my hand.

I drove through the mist without a plan and ended up at the cliffs, the spot where my dad—

I can't talk about my dad yet.

Let's talk about the aftermath.

The short version of the aftermath goes like this: I lost the election to my former flame Brad, I almost flunked out of school, and Stanford rejected me.

Chris, meanwhile, came out, chopped her hair off, bought some Doc Martens, started doing slam poetry to express her feelings, and was awarded a scholarship to UPenn. Until that point, she responded to both Chris and Christina. After that point, she made Chris official. I avoided her like she was contagious for the rest of the year.

Even though she'd never admitted to taking the photo or to spreading the flyers, she was the only one who could have done it. No one else could have taken the photo because no one else was there that night, and no one else wanted to ruin me as much as Chris Dane did.

CHAPTER 20

stevie

Wiener watched me as I pulled on my shoes, his doggy face tilting right, then left, then right again. The next part of my getting-ready process was to grab my headphones from the little box by the door where I always kept them, but this morning, they weren't there. How could they not be there? They were always there, as in *always*, as in not once had they not been inside this box, which I had now opened at least seven times. Either (a) it was fine, I'd go without them, or (b) my life was falling apart. I decided it was (c) both, then put my hand on the doorknob and said, "Stay, Wiener."

Wiener tilted his head.

"Do *not* go outside."

I opened the door.

He ran outside.

This turned out not to be a big deal. Wiener did his morning business at the foot of the trash hedge and then came right back. The drama rose again when he skittered into the kitchen and started barking, and the drama subsided when I realized that I should feed him. The tinny sound of the hard food pellets hitting the metallic bowl was like a wind chime in a storm. One minute later—and six minutes behind schedule—I was walking across the street to the beach, enjoying the drop in temperature and the fresh salty air on my face.

I started jogging once I'd reached the sand, same as always. It was harder without music. Normally, European techno beats blasted into my ears so loud that there were no thoughts in my head, only the impulse to run faster, maybe to run away from the singers screaming at me in languages I didn't understand. The sand was so cold and dense under my feet that it could have been snow.

At the last lifeguard tower, I veered toward the boardwalk, and this was when I realized that my shoe was untied. I propped my foot up to retie it on the beach wall that said NO BONFIRES—and that's when somebody tapped me on the shoulder.

I turned around to find Chris Dane—except it wasn't Chris Dane.

It was Brad Rose with a surfboard under his arm.

My first thought?

Sign.

Then I remembered that I'd told him I jogged here, so maybe it wasn't.

"Yo," Brad said, and kissed me lightly on the cheek.

"Brad!"

"This might sound nuts," Brad said, running his fingers through his hair, which was only slightly longer than Chris's, "but do you want to go out sometime? Like, round two, adult-style? Maybe George's?"

This was exactly what I had wanted to happen, so I pretended I didn't want it at all. "I usually don't date my clients, Brad."

Brad's smile flattened to a line. "Okay."

"But I'll make an exception for you."

"Awesome!" His eyes sparkled. "Pick you up tomorrow at eight? Text me your address?"

"I'll do it right now." As I typed it in, I said, "I can't believe you're going to pick me up. Nobody has picked me up for a date in . . . I don't even know how long."

"Chivalry," Brad said. He kissed me on the cheek again—the light scratch of his stubble reminded me of a loofah—and then he was jogging toward the water like the model in an Acqua di Giò ad, but the California version. Or whatever, he was just David Beckham.

Shower, dress, makeup.

Who am I?

Who am I now?

What about now?

I turned around, lifted my shirt, checked my scar.

Why was I always doing this?

I think it was because I had the secret hope that one day, I'd turn around and somehow it would be gone.

I am La Jolla's number one decluttering guru.

I am La Jolla's number one decluttering guru.

I am La Jolla's number one decluttering guru.

Thoughts running through my head as I said my affirmations:

If you love yourself, then you will attract love.

A partner.

A long-term relationship.

A house on the water.

Stella's paper city.

Chris.

Don't think about Dad.

———

At 7:25, Bonnie came out of her room dressed in another lovely outfit from the mall and said, "Good morning, Inspector."

"What?"

"Inspector Gadget, the Oreo Cookie—"

"Why are you up so early?"

"I'm here to amaze you." Bonnie curtsied. "Did you see we that we have eleven hundred followers this morning?"

"Really?"

"Our scores on Organizely are still the same, but I did some math," Bonnie said. Then she started talking numbers. The actual numbers didn't register, but what it boiled down to was that we didn't need that many more five-star reviews to win, and even if we got 4.9s it would still make a substantial impact. But in order to do that, we needed more clients.

"So I booked two more consultations for this afternoon," Bonnie said. "One young person and one old person."

"What!"

"Are you mad?"

"No! I'm—Bonnie, that's great! Thank you!"

What I was thinking: *It's all happening, Stevie. The world is opening up for you.*

I was also thinking: *Bonnie is so on point this morning. Why?*

"Everett's house really inspired you, didn't it?"

"It did!"

We were now in the kitchen, where Bonnie was making her winter wonderland breakfast and I was checking my phone. I went to Instagram, where, yes, we had 1,230 followers and—

"Oh my god."

"What?"

"Mom friended us."

"*Our* mom?"

"And she posted a selfie with a margarita. At El Ranchero?"

Bonnie hovered over my shoulder. "Okay, no, she needs to delete that."

The picture was blurry, but the margarita looked—honestly, it looked kind of good.

Bonnie took a pensive bite of yogurt. "Since when does Mom take selfies?"

"Since when does Mom sign up for Instagram?"

"And the dolls-as-a-couple thing?" Bonnie said.

"I know."

"Something's going on with her." Bonnie re-illuminated her phone screen. "Also, why did she take a selfie if she was out with Donna?"

CHAPTER 21

stevie

Let me tell you why Chris Dane wanted to ruin me in high school.

But first let me tell you that technically, I did win the election, and by a landslide. High school students weren't going to take me down for doing coke. They were doing coke, too, and most of the ones who weren't wanted to try it. In retrospect, maybe it was also the people who wanted to make out with their best friends who voted for me, and my advice about that would have been: sure, do it, but first make sure your best friend isn't going to stab you in the back.

What I wanted to say to everyone who saw the flyer: *We were experimenting!*

Was it true? I honestly didn't know. Chris and I made out all the time, but only when we were wasted, so it was hard to know if it counted or not. It was hard to know how I felt about it. It was hard to know what I wanted.

Chris knew what she wanted. She wanted to hold my hand at the movies sometimes, and that was not okay. Unless

I was drunk, I wasn't interested. I liked to think of us as best friends who made out kind of accidentally. It was an accident that kept happening, yes, but we didn't need to plan our futures around it. We were young and stupid. It was a phase, it didn't mean anything, I barely remembered it most of the time.

In the weeks leading up to the election, Chris had started to want more from me, and my reaction was to give her less. "What if we didn't drink tonight?" she asked, her big eyes wanting to take up more space, wanting to swallow me whole. "We could do, like, a healthy spa night? And eat salads and rub each other's feet?"

I wanted to kill her. We had a code, and she was breaking it. We'd never talked about any code, but I assumed we both understood its terms and conditions in the same way. I said hell no to spa night. Although what I really said was, "I have to study." So there was a lot we weren't saying.

Eating lunch together became fraught. Normally, it was fun to gather with our friends on the quad to exchange gossip and complain about teachers while having this tension, this other life that nobody knew about, this secret. To everyone else, we were best friends, inseparable, sort of glamorous, high-achieving. And I wanted to keep it that way.

The one pact we had discussed was that we would not tell anyone that we were doing drugs. I remember saying, "Not even weed. If we're at a party, I'm saying no." Chris thought I was being overly cautious, but she went along with it.

At parties, we'd drink a few light beers. Then we'd go back to Chris's house because her parents were always in

Greece and we'd attack their liquor cabinet. We'd take three shots of vodka in a row. Then I'd set out some lines for us. I'd found a dealer at UCSD who overcharged me but was always punctual.

By the morning I arrived at school to find the flyers, Chris and I had been "on a break" for five days. These were her words, which sounded like relationship words, which just made me want to kill her more. After I'd said no to spa night and to movie night and to all other plans that sounded like marriage, Chris had given me an ultimatum: "Either be my girlfriend or we need to take a break."

An hour after I left school, I was still sitting in the car at the cliffs, and Chris called me.

"Oh my god, I'm so worried about you," she said. "I can't believe we haven't spoken in *five days*!"

My first thought?

Chris had orchestrated a catastrophe not so that I would lose the election, but so that I would need her.

"Don't call me again," I said, and hung up.

In the weeks that followed, I went back over the facts so many times. I stared at the flyer, trying to figure it out. The photo had been taken in Chris's living room. Chris must have placed the camera on the mantel, which explained the long angle. Chris often used the timer function on her camera in those days. The photo had been taken with a flash. A flash is a pretty clear alert that a photo is being taken.

But I didn't remember any flash.

This was the one part that was missing from the story: my memory.

I must have blacked out.

CHAPTER 22

STEVIE

I often did this thing where I promised myself I would not share a piece of information. I'd be like, *Self, do not share this.* And then one second later, I was saying the thing I'd just sworn I would not say.

We were on our way to Lauren Strong's, climbing the part of La Jolla Shores Drive that curves through the eucalyptus trees like a lazy river, and I said, "I have a date with Brad Rose tomorrow night."

Bonnie rolled her lips together. "I don't think that's a strong choice, but I'm here to support you in your choices even if they suck."

I don't know why it took me until then to figure it out. "Oh my god, you're jealous. *You* want to date Brad."

"What!"

"If we don't work out, then you can have him."

"I'm *not* jealous, dude," Bonnie said. "Not even close."

I didn't believe her. After that, every time Bonnie expressed her disapproval of Brad, I thought, *Oh, she's just jealous.* I was thrilled to have found the reason why she didn't want me to date him. It all made sense. Bonnie had been jealous of me dating Brad in high school, and now here she was, newly single and jealous again.

We kept driving. More eucalyptus trees. And palm trees. The sidewalk-less streets in the Farms. I thought, *Bonnie does not need to know about my plans with Chris. Nope, I'm definitely not going to tell her.*

One second later: "Also I'm having dinner with Chris tonight."

And: "I don't want to get my hopes up, but I'm hoping she might apologize. Maybe she needed a day to think about it, you know? I think she was caught off guard before."

"And if she does apologize, then you'll forgive her?" Bonnie asked.

"Of course!"

"You won't still be mad?"

"I don't think so."

"You won't punish her?"

"No, I'll be happy. I'm so sick of thinking about this! And talking about this! It's eats up so much space in my brain you have no idea. But I can't let it go. I mean, you get it, right? It's the unsolved mystery of my life."

"I have to tell you something, Stevie," Bonnie said.

Her use of my name made it sound serious. "What?"

Bonnie tugged at her hair. "You might be pissed."

"What did you do?"

"You might be really pissed."

"Bonnie, tell me what you did."

"This morning?" Bonnie began. "While you were on your run?"

I waited.

"I was going to fill your Sutter Homes with water, but instead I just threw them away for you." Bonnie opened the center console so I could see.

I kept my eyes on the road. If my hands clenched the steering wheel, then they didn't clench it very hard, and my jaw didn't tighten that much either, because you know what I thought it was?

A sign.

Also, I'd begun to imagine Chris getting in my car, and if that happened and she found the wine stash, I'd be ashamed.

"You know what, Bonnie?" I said. "Thank you."

———

Lauren opened the door and said the word "hey" in five syllables.

"Hee-ee-ee-ee-eey."

Then, to Bonnie: "Who are *you*?"

"The sister," Bonnie said.

"You're a redhead!"

"And you're a repeat offender," Bonnie said. "Stevie told me in the car."

"Ugh, I *know*. It's like abundance on overdrive. Which is so weird. You'd think that more would make you feel like more, but really it just points out that all your problems are internal."

Lauren rolled her eyes for Bonnie. Then, suddenly frantic, or at least three degrees more frantic than usual, she grabbed my wrist.

"By the way, Stevie, I have not had *any* wine since I last saw you. I've been wanting it *so* bad, but then I'm like, 'No, if Stevie Green can be on a cleanse, then so can I.'"

"A cleanse," Bonnie said, not unlike a cop who was repeating a clue.

"Are you on one, too?" Lauren asked.

"I don't drink that much," Bonnie said.

"No, me neither," Lauren said. "I would call myself a *moderate* drinker. Although Vincent likes to drink, so it's hard not to drink when I'm with him, but I think I'm getting better at saying no."

As we followed Lauren into her house, she told Bonnie more about Vincent. "And he has a job, but he never has to go to an office, so it's convenient. Have you ever cheated on anyone?"

"Yes," Bonnie said.

"Really?" I was stunned.

"Dwight and I were together for *seventeen* years."

"Todd and I have only been together for eight," Lauren said. "And it *can't* end. Which is why you're here." She turned to Bonnie. "We're on the brink of divorce because he's a minimalist and I'm not."

"Looks pretty minimalist in here," Bonnie said, eyeing the modern couch and the floating staircase and the long bare hallway that led to the garage.

Lauren sighed. "Illusion."

Determined to leap back from the brink of divorce, Lauren bid a fast adieu to three-fourths of her makeup collection, all seventeen tennis rackets, thirty-five pairs of sneakers, and every piece of clothing that she'd kept out of guilt, including the skinny jeans from her twenties, the shirts with the stains on them that she always planned to fix but never had, the scratchy scarves she'd bought in destinations now forgotten, and the hideous gifts that had been given to her by friends and family—but not including the hideous gifts she'd received from Todd, because she felt too guilty getting rid of those. Todd was her *husband*, and also, his gifts were eco-friendly.

"And wearing sustainable clothes is just, like, the right thing to do, right?" she asked herself. Or maybe she was asking us. It wasn't clear.

She kneaded a pair of pin-striped chinos between her fingers and explained how they'd been made of recycled cotton somewhere far away. "Maybe South Africa? I forget what Todd said."

I could tell just by looking at them that those chinos had the consistency of cardboard. In an attempt to wake Lauren up from her autopilot existence, I set my hands on her bony shoulders. "Lauren, are these chinos *you*?"

"I don't know that they're *not* me," Lauren said. "But I don't know that they're *me* me either. I guess it depends on where I'm planning on going."

"When was the last time you wore them?" Bonnie asked.

"Never," Lauren whispered.

We waited in silence until eventually, she loosened her grip and let the hideous pants fall into the bag Bonnie was holding out for her. Once they'd landed silently, a smile spread out across her face. "Whoa. That felt *good*."

With the smile still on her face, Lauren got rid of many more garments after that, and then we went up to Finny's room, where her happy attitude took a turn.

Bonnie, upon seeing the child's stuffed animal zoo, shared her knee-jerk reaction. "This is unhealthy."

Lauren's face went slack. "Oh."

I suggested that Lauren keep only one animal for each letter of the alphabet. "So you'll still have twenty-six," I explained.

Lauren tentatively agreed—"Oka-aa-aa-ay"—then backtracked. "But the ape *and* the antelope are both super cute."

"The ape isn't cute, sorry," Bonnie said.

"Fine." Lauren chucked the ape at Bonnie, who caught it without a problem. Then she melted to the floor with an "Uuuugggghhh."

Was Lauren kind of a child in some ways? Was her childishness suddenly more apparent in the presence of her child's stuff?

Yes. But digging deeper into these questions was not my job. All I cared about was getting her off the floor before she lost all momentum. And so I invented a story about hope.

"Lauren," I said, "in San Diego right now, there's a family with not a lot of money. The parents shop at Goodwill. Imagine them finding this porcupine or that cheetah and bringing it home to a kid who has zero stuffed animals. Imagine how good that kid is going to feel."

Lauren blinked at me several times. "That was me. I was that kid. My parents shopped at secondhand stores." She gazed at the animals with new detachment. "Oh my god. I have to give back. It's like . . . karma."

After the word "karma" had been spoken, Lauren went on a humanistic tear.

"Let's donate all but two of the Vespas to charity. And you know what? Finny only needs one Fisher-Price car."

We rounded up all the rejects and watched Lauren make the call to Goodwill to schedule a pickup. When she was done, she untied her bun and shook her head out in a sexy way.

"I kind of want a glass of wine right now to celebrate, but because of you, Stevie, I'm not going to do it."

Before I could say anything, Lauren threw her fragile arms around me and squeezed, and in this equation, I was the sturdy one, which was nice.

———

That afternoon, we did consultations for four new clients.

Later, Bonnie would describe them all as lonely, anxious women with a skewed perception of the universe, and she was probably right, because who isn't lonely and anxious and appallingly wrong about reality?

I think this definition fits pretty much everyone.

———

First on the list was Fancy Desai, thirty-five, whose home looked like a flea market after an earthquake. Photographs of asymmetrical haircuts hung in a jumbled non-pattern on the wall. The cushions on the couch were several different colors and textures. Overlapping rugs littered the floor, and yes, their designs were clashing. If Fancy Desai's house were a sound, it would have been the sound of someone screaming.

"I was trying to be unique," Fancy explained, "but I think I went too far."

"What's with the hair pictures?" Bonnie asked.

"I'm a hair witch," Fancy said. "Hair speaks to me. I cut all my friends' hair in the backyard."

What was Fancy's hair like? It was astoundingly boring: long and brown and parted down the middle. I took this to mean that she possessed a classic and ordered spirit inside of her that was yearning to come out.

"I see what you need," I told her. "And soon, you're going to get it."

———————

After Fancy, there was Veronica Wu, forty-six, who had a bunch of taxidermy in her house and a small army of jeans that no longer fit.

"Will I ever be a size two again?" she moaned.

Bonnie and I were smart enough not to answer this question, and Veronica never answered it either. She toggled her pearl earring and looked at the stuffed boar in the corner and said, "I tried to get rid of them by myself. I even put them in the garage. But then I brought them back in. So that's why you're here."

———————

Stacy P was another woman with too many clothes. She was also a paralegal who freaking hated being a paralegal but freaking loved The F, which was what she called Forever 21, her favorite store.

No, Stacy P had never heard of sustainable fashion. Yes, she knew she was a shopaholic. "The clothes are for auditions," she said while smacking her Bubblicious. "What I really want to be is J.Lo."

Stacy P had organized her clothes in piles on the floor according to color, "because this is how The F displays their merch," she explained. "Like a rainbow."

"I can't even think in here," Bonnie said.

"I can't think in here either," Stacy P admitted.

We told her not to worry, we'd be back to clean her up, and in the car driving away from her house, Bonnie asked me a good question: "Do you ever feel energetically compromised by these people?"

———————

Polly Johnson, seventy-five, lived in a modest house on an extravagantly built-up street.

"We bought in the sixties," she said.

The interior was many shades of brown—light brown, dark brown, dusty brown, cracked leather brown, termite-nibbled brown—and it smelled like a mysterious combination of Pine-Sol and wet mulch.

She took us on a short tour, then told us that her husband, Ed, had died recently, and that she was having trouble parting with his belongings.

I said the same thing to her that I'd said to my mother when we were packing up Moonridge. "The first half of life is about acquiring, and the second half is about letting go."

Polly was staring at me, her eyes flickering back and forth and back and forth.

"I *know* you."

"You do?"

"Yes, but where do I know you from?"

Honestly, and maybe this was unfair, but I thought she possibly had a touch of dementia, especially when she said, "Green," a bunch of times.

"Green . . . Green . . . Green."

"Green is a popular name," I said, moving toward the door as fast as I could without giving Polly the impression that I was desperate to escape. "You might be thinking of somebody else?"

"No," Polly said.

I was sure she was thinking of somebody else.

"We'll be back next week," I said, and flashed a smile. "Maybe by then, you'll remember."

CHAPTER 23

kit

"I'm addicted to the likes," I said to Bonnie.

"Normal," she said.

While waiting for our takeout to arrive, I'd given her my phone, and now she was adding new pictures to Instagram for me. Watching her, I felt a wave of hope. Maybe my career would expand again. A second resurgence. I thought I'd peaked in the nineties, but perhaps I was wrong. Perhaps the peak was ahead of me.

"Hashtag art, hashtag La Jolla, hashtag Kit Green."

"Hashtag resurgence," I added.

Bonnie typed it in. As I watch her hit *Post*, I felt a flutter inside. Would people like it?

"And now we're going to delete this," Bonnie said, clicking on my photo from El Ranchero. "Okay? It's too blurry."

"Okay," I agreed. The picture reminded me of Douglas, and I didn't want to want to remember him anyway.

"Also, where was Donna?"

It took me a moment to remember my lie. "Oh, she was in the bathroom."

Bonnie handed me my phone. Then she stared at me.

"What, Bonnie?"

Bonnie blinked. Then she blinked again. Then she said, "I wasn't going to tell you this, and don't tell Stevie you know, like absolutely *do not*, Mom, but I found wine in her car."

"No."

"I threw it away," she said.

Suddenly, I felt like I was spinning. Suddenly, I wished I lived alone again. I couldn't bear another catastrophe. A woman my age should be enjoying her life, not worrying about her children's lives. Maybe Douglas was right. My kids shouldn't be living with me. It wasn't normal. It wasn't good. But it did feel like my fault. They were broken birds, unable to fly the nest because I hadn't taught them any life skills.

CHAPTER 24

stevie

"I can't apologize for something I didn't do," Chris said.

It was seven p.m. at Spice & Rice, and we hadn't even sat down yet. I'd told myself to wait before bringing it up, but I couldn't. Right after Chris said, "How are you?" I blurted it out: "Please just admit that you're responsible for those flyers."

Now I was checking her eyes to see if she was lying. I was waiting for her to look up and to the left, which is where people look when they lie. Or was it the right?

But she didn't look up.

The hostess, a raspy-voiced brunette with a nose piercing, said, "Your table's ready."

I thought about leaving. I imagined myself saying, *I have to go*, and walking out.

"You coming?" Chris asked, walking toward the table already.

I just watched her for a moment—her good jeans, her white sneakers, the way she carried herself with such certainty—and then, deeply unsure and slightly annoyed, I followed her.

We sat down.

You can leave at any point, I reminded myself. *You don't have to stay here.*

I was handed a menu.

"And the wine menu," the hostess said.

"No thanks," Chris said. "I'm good."

"I'm good, too," I echoed.

Chris looked at me with her big, calm eyes. "Your mom told me you stopped drinking," she said.

"I'm on a cleanse."

Chris smiled. "Love a cleanse."

She didn't tell me she'd been sober for ten years. She didn't mention her meetings. She studied the menu. I already knew I wanted a green papaya salad and a side of sticky rice. That was my stock Thai restaurant order. I never changed it.

"Panang curry . . ." Chris said, mostly to herself.

"Chris, I don't know if I can do this," I said.

"Stevie, can I ask you a question?"

"Yes."

"What if you're wrong?"

I said nothing. Chris slid her fuzzy wool coat off her shoulders and hung it on the back of her chair. I left my coat on just in case I decided to leave. I was perched on the edge of my seat, ready to bolt. Chris scooted her chair forward. Somewhere in the restaurant was a fountain. I could hear the faint sound of water falling into water.

"You want to know who I think did it?" she said.

"Who?"

"Brad Rose."

I laughed. "That's too obvious. He was the one running against me! And Brad Rose is harmless! It doesn't fit his character profile."

"But it fits mine?" Chris laughed. "Stevie, remember when you dumped Brad? Remember how upset he was?"

"He wasn't *that* upset. He won the election and got a new girlfriend. Kathy, or whatever her name was."

"Kathy Malkin, who had to hear about how you broke Brad's heart for the rest of senior year, which you might not know because you essentially stopped coming to school."

"Wait, really?"

"Really," Chris said. "And Stevie? People aren't harmless when you hurt them."

The words I left unsaid: *Didn't I hurt you?*

The server returned to the table. "What can I get for you?"

I ordered reluctantly, and Chris ordered pleasantly, and after the server had left with our menus, I said, "Anyway, Brad hired us to declutter his house. 'Us' being me and Bonnie. We're working together now. Maybe my mom told you?"

"She did, yeah," Chris said. And then: "How's *Brad*?"

"I mean, he's still hot. And this morning he asked me out and I said yes. Isn't that hilarious?"

"Wow," Chris said, suddenly becoming interested in the orchid on the table. She reached out to touch one of its leaves. "Are you—actually, sorry, never mind."

"What?"

Chris pondered my face. I felt like she was examining me. I didn't like it. "I guess I was just wondering how you identify now."

I kept my body as still as possible as I searched for a comical retort to this question.

The best I could come up with was this: "I identify as a person." Then I laughed. It was horrible. I could tell Chris felt sorry for me.

"Honestly, I think Brad might be the one who got away. It would just make such a good story if we ended up together, wouldn't it?"

"Totally," Chris said in a louder voice than the one she'd been using before. "It would make a great story. Unless he was the one who made those flyers. Have you asked him?"

"Of course not."

Chris stared at me. And kept staring at me. I thought I was just going to sit there and do nothing, but then somehow I was pulling out my phone and narrating the message to Brad as I typed it: "Brad, this is silly, but I have a question. Did you make those flyers in high school?"

One second later, he wrote back: No!

"He said no," I reported to Chris.

"Great," she said, but she didn't seem satisfied.

CHAPTER 25

chris

After dinner, I got in my car and cried. I cried because we were never going to be together. And I cried because even though I didn't want to love her, I somehow still did. I decided the only thing to do was to put some space between us.

That night, my house felt lonelier than usual. It was a beautiful house, but what was the point of having a beautiful house if you had no one to share it with? Even though I didn't want to, I imagined Stevie in my house. I imagined her sitting on the couch with me. I imagined her laughing.

So I took out my phone and wrote to several women on Hinge: Heidi, Sam, Tilda, Maria.

Hey, how's your night going?

I sent the message four times. And then I promised myself that if Stevie wrote to me, I would not write back.

stevie

Am I straight? Am I not?

These were my thoughts as I drove home, and yes, I'd had these thoughts before. Of course I had. But I didn't know the correct answer, and I resented the pressure to figure it out. What was the point of labeling yourself beyond "person"? Couldn't I just be a person? The other part of this story, the part I never mentioned to anyone: I'd never slept with a woman sober, and I'd never slept with a man sober. And this meant that if the choices were:

a. Straight
b. Not straight
c. Not enugh information

Then I was circling C.

I did not have enough information.

I'd pulled into the gas station without formally making the choice to go there. It just kind of happened. I checked the gas tank. I didn't need gas. Maybe I needed a bottle of water, though.

Inside, the gas station was lit like a lightning strike. Electrically white. I grabbed a bottle of water from the refrigerated section. And then, as a last-minute thought—was it a last-minute thought?—I grabbed three mini chardonnays from the dusty bottom of a shelf. It was one of those moments when you think, *If anybody saw me right now, I would die.*

Nobody saw me. I paid. I left. I stashed the bottles in the pocket behind the driver's seat this time so Bonnie wouldn't find them.

CHAPTER 27

stevie

I found Bonnie in the kitchen at six o'clock in the morning.

"You're up early," I said.

"Couldn't sleep," Bonnie said. "I'm going to surf while you run. I need my abs back."

What I didn't say: *I think I'm a positive influence on you now.*

What I did say: "Chris refuses to apologize."

Bonnie looked up at the ceiling for a second, then back at me. "I'm sorry."

"She thinks Brad did it," I said. "Which is absurd."

Bonnie turned to grab a mug from the shelf. I took a sip of my coffee. Wiener walked in a circle three times, then curled up in his onion bagel dog bed. I took another sip of coffee.

"Chris Dane is never going to apologize to me," I said. "It's just never going to happen. So I either need to let this go or beg her for an apology that I'm never going to get for the rest of my life. Which—I can't do that. She was like,

'What if you're wrong?' But if she didn't do it and Brad didn't do it, which I know is true because I texted him right there at the table—"

"Wait, you texted Brad to ask if he did it?"

"Yeah, Chris kind of dared me to. Or she didn't *dare* me to, but—"

"And Brad said he didn't do it."

"Of course he didn't do it! And maybe I *am* wrong about Chris. Maybe I had some enemy I didn't even know about? Maybe somebody snuck in and took the picture. Which is possible? But I'm still like, *Who? Who, who, who? Who ruined my life?* But I'm *still* letting them ruin my life! Like right now, by my talking about this, they're still ruining my life. And I'm *letting* them. I feel insane."

Bonnie gave me a very sad look. "I'm sorry."

"I have to let it go. I *have* to let it go. I can't talk about this anymore. Okay, starting today, I'm not going to talk about this anymore. The best revenge is living well, right? I need to become number one. *We* need to become number one. That's it."

"That's it," Bonnie echoed. "And whoever did this to you, I'm sure they feel like an asshole now. So they're already suffering. You don't even need to worry about it."

"That's true. I'm sure they hate themselves."

"They definitely hate themselves," Bonnie said. "A lot."

I ran that morning like I was running away from something. The *something* I imagined behind me was a shark or a leopard or a fanged bear. I turned my techno music up louder than usual. I turned it up so loud that all thoughts of Chris were blasted out of my head.

Well, mostly.

Bonnie and I had planned to meet at home, but thirty-eight minutes later, when I'd circled back to her surf spot, I stopped. I sat down on the damp, compacted sand between the washed-up florets of kelp and watched as she leaned back into a wave and then cut straight up and then leaned back again, the tube crashing behind her all the time, the white trails she made swallowed up by its curve. I thought about how it must have felt to trust like that, and about the beauty of nature, which seemed remarkable every time you remembered it.

It also seemed remarkable that I'd actually sat down. Did this count as meditating? I thought it basically did.

———

The shower. The Oreo Cookie outfit. The mirror. The scar. *Who am I now?*

I invited Bonnie to do the mantra with me that day. "With your hands on your hips like Wonder Woman," I explained. "It sends a message to your brain that you're powerful."

We are La Jolla's number one decluttering gurus.

We are La Jolla's number one decluttering gurus.

We are La Jolla's number one decluttering gurus.

Bonnie wore a dress that was reminiscent of her poncho, but not offensively reminiscent. This is what I thought as I stood facing her in the living room: *Bonnie is changing. And I am changing. Change is not only possible. It's inevitable.*

The Pilot G2 roller, the legal pad, the *project*.

But first I checked my phone.

"Fifteen hundred Instagram followers," I said, and Bonnie, who was getting faster at making her yogurt wonderland, said, "I know." She'd posted new photos from the shoot. We looked good. Better than good. We looked like an ad.

Next I opened Organizely and—

"Ah!"

"What?"

"Lauren gave us five stars, and now we're at a four-point-seven!"

The scores were now 4.7 to 4.8, which meant that we were encroaching. It was only a matter of time before Ursula de Santis became obsolete.

"Let's take a selfie," Bonnie said, already extending her arm up and out.

So we did. And Bonnie posted it. And somebody commented that they loved us, somebody I didn't even know, and I felt momentarily whole.

CHAPTER 28

stevie

Stella opened the door wearing a silk jumpsuit that looked like it had been poured over her body. When she said my name in her deep voice, I thought it sounded like chocolate.

"Stevie."

"And Bonnie," Bonnie said, extending a hand. "We're sisters."

"You are?" Stella said. "I never would have guessed that."

"Yeah, Stevie used to call me the mailman's child," Bonnie said. "Because I'm the only redhead in the family."

"Bon-nie," I said like an old woman on a sitcom who was slapping her thigh.

Stella laughed quietly, then invited us in.

———

Why did Stella make me so nervous? This was the question I was trying to answer the entire time we were in there.

I came to a few conclusions.

She made me nervous because she had the life that I wanted but didn't have yet.

She made me nervous because of the way she looked at me with such astonishing kindness.

She made me nervous because in that silk jumpsuit, she was one degree away from being naked.

So I tried to look only at her face and not her body when I spoke to her. It was hard. Have you ever tried to look *only* at someone's face? It's impossible. What ended up happening was that I looked away a lot.

I set my eyes on the bluish chandelier hanging over the staircase and said, "Let's start with your paper city."

I'd forgotten that "paper city" was a thing I'd said only to myself. Stella had never heard that term before.

"Paper city?" She smiled. "That's great."

We went to the guest room. Bonnie took one look at the paper city and said, "Okay, no."

"When I was a kid, I used to keep all my movie stubs," Stella told us. "And all my homework assignments. I don't really know why, though, because I never looked at them again. Funny how we don't change very much, isn't it?"

The first folder Stella opened contained the registration for a car she no longer owned. The next folder contained documents belonging to a fraud case she'd won in 1992. "I remember this guy. He opened a bunch of credit cards using his brother's social security number and then bought several boats."

At first, Stella wanted to go through the contents of

every folder. Then she decided to only look at the labels. Half an hour later, the look became a quick glance. "No to this, no thank you, goodbye," she said, tossing the folders into the trash bag held out for her by Bonnie, who reminded her she was doing the right thing.

"You're doing the right thing."

"I'm already getting tired," Stella said.

I passed her another folder while trying not to look at her body in that jumpsuit, and said, "That's normal."

Five minutes later, Stella got a paper cut. She winced, then looked at the paper city and said, "Maybe we should just throw the rest of this away?"

"What's the worst that could happen?" I said.

"I'd worry that later, I might need to reference something and it wouldn't be here?"

"Like the movie stubs you saved as a kid that you never referenced again?"

Stella laughed. "Right."

So the three of us started filling up trash bags like it was our reason for being born. I was relieved, as usual, to be presented with a tangible way to move forward: put the folders in the bag.

The paper maze was disassembled layer by layer. Bonnie snapped pics to track our progress. We hauled everything out to the street because tomorrow was recycling day. Stella pushed her glasses higher up on her elegant nose and said, "I feel lighter already."

———

Upstairs, Stella showed Bonnie the same picture of her and Marianne that she'd shown me before, and Bonnie said, "She's hot."

"Isn't she?" Stella said as we followed her into the walk-in closet.

Everything in that closet was beautiful. A mix of smart pantsuits and dresses hung on heavy wooden hangers like art. "Marianne and I both wear a lot of this stuff," she said, pulling at the sleeve of a crisp striped shirt.

"I want to be gay," Bonnie said wistfully. "You get double the wardrobe."

Stella smiled. "It is one perk."

I thought about laughing, but decided to keep my eyes focused on the clothes instead.

Stella ended up getting rid of two dresses and a fabulous black vest with a tie in the back. As she let the garments slip from her fingers into the bag, Bonnie said, "All of this would look amazing on Stevie. You guys have the same body."

"Oh, Stevie," Stella said, "please take whatever you want. Take it all."

"Thank you," I said like it didn't matter, because honestly, it felt like it mattered a lot.

"Thank *you*," Stella said.

"Our pleasure," I said, and tried not to blush.

Stella smiled. "Come on, I'll walk you out."

We followed her out of the closet and down the stairs, and just as we were about to reach the front door, Marianne and another woman walked through it.

"Hey, you must be the declutterers!" Marianne said, and then we all introduced ourselves. Marianne's eyes were very green, and her movements, like Stella's, were effortless. The other woman was named Lex. She was thirty-two, she told us, and taller than me, and she carried herself like a snowboarder. She had an authentic way of smiling that creased all the lines on her face, which somehow made her look both older and younger than she was. She was smiling as she shook my hand with genuine feeling.

"Nice to meet you."

"Nice to meet you, too."

Then Marianne said, "Stay for iced tea?"

Bonnie RSVP'd us on the spot. "We'd love to!"

A few minutes later, we were all sitting in the living room with our iced teas, and I was watching Marianne place a bowl of edamame crackers on the coffee table.

I didn't know what to say, so I went with a popular question. "How did you two meet?"

"At a bar," Marianne said.

"A grungy dive bar in Spain." Stella smiled as she brought a cracker to her lips.

"I've never met anyone good in a bar," Lex said.

I said, "Me neither," then ate a cracker just to have something to do, or to be polite. I wasn't sure which.

"I saw your files outside," Marianne kissed Stella on the cheek. "Proud of you, babe."

Then, to us, she said, "You have no idea how long I've been waiting for this day. Thank you."

We said, "You're welcome," and "No problem," and "Happy to help."

And then Lex turned to me. "Hey, can I get your number?" she said. "Here, you can put it in my phone."

She handed me her phone. I typed everything in and handed it back.

Lex smiled with her whole face.

"Call anytime," I said. "We can set up a consultation."

Lex uncrossed her legs and sat back. "I will."

CHAPTER 29

bonnie

In the car, I told Stevie she was an idiot.

"Lex doesn't want a consultation. She wants to ask you out."

For the record, I've always thought my sister was into women. Like, no-brainer. But you can't *say* that to someone. So I'd never said anything.

"Ask me out?"

"Stevie, you're blind."

But Stevie wasn't paying attention. Or she was paying more attention to the clothes Stella had given her than she was to me. She'd taken one of the dresses out of the bag, and now she was petting it like it was precious.

"I'm going to wear this tonight on my date with Brad," she said.

I could have told her everything right then. If I had, it might have saved us all from the horrible drama that came next. But I didn't. I swallowed the lump in my throat instead and opened Instagram. After we were number one, I would tell her.

brad

What did I want?

I wanted Stevie. I'd always wanted her. I thought she was the hottest woman alive, and probably the smartest, too. She was the first woman I ever fell in love with. I think, in a way, I never stopped being in love with her. That's what happens with your first love, right? You love them forever.

When my buddy Patrick mentioned that she was back in town doing this decluttering thing, I was like, "What? I thought Stevie Green was in Paris or something." I never expected to see her again. In my head, she'd married some French dude and was living happily ever after in a beret. I spent like a week trying to decide if I should contact her or not. I sort of had this feeling that if I did, she'd break my heart again. But then I decided that the same person can't break your heart twice, and also, where was my positivity? What if it turned out to be great?

So I dumped my girlfriend, Rachel. I probably would have dumped her anyway. She wore fake nails and carried her Yorkie in her purse. I think that tells you everything you need to know about Rachel. We just weren't really on the same wavelength.

After Stevie came to my house, I knew I'd made the right choice by dumping Rachel. Rachel was a zero compared to Stevie. Not even on the map. I could have asked Stevie out in a text, but I thought finding her on the beach would be better.

Anyway, there was a lot riding on that first date for me. I did a double swish with the mouthwash. I bought flowers. I got there five minutes early and waited it out. I didn't want to seem too eager.

As I walked up to her door, I was thinking that, yeah, it was weird that she'd quizzed me about the high school thing.

But "weird" didn't mean "bad," necessarily.

Right?

CHAPTER 31

stevie

At eight p.m. on the dot, Brad Rose knocked three times on my front door, and I felt like my life was a rom-com.

I was sitting on the couch in Stella's black velvet dress and the only pair of heels I owned. I don't know why I wore heels, because my whole game was to be comfortable, but I guess I just thought that I should.

I checked my phone again. Earlier, I'd written to Chris. How was your day?

She still hadn't responded.

I wasn't upset about that. Was I? No, I wasn't upset.

I got up and opened the door at a casual speed to find Brad in a blue sports jacket holding a well-chosen flower arrangement wrapped in parchment paper.

"Hey," he said, and when he smiled, with one side of his mouth rising up before the other, I sank into that familiar place again: *Oh yeah, I know you.*

"How is the lovely couple this evening?" the waiter sang in a regaling voice that made me think he'd been on Broadway once. He was older, with gelled black hair and a toothy grin. And he'd just called us a couple. "Can I start you off with a glass of champagne?"

Brad held out an upturned palm like he was offering me a future on a small invisible platter.

And then he said, "Bottle?"

His eyes twinkled in the low light. The din of the restaurant got louder. The waiter shifted on his feet. I felt tiny as I practiced the words, *I'm on a cleanse*.

"Veuve Clicquot?" the waiter said, like it had already been decided. "And a dozen oysters?"

"Stevie, you eat oysters, right?" Brad looked hopeful.

I heard myself say, *I'm on a cleanse*.

What I said out loud was, "I love oysters."

The waiter said, "Wonderful."

Brad said, "Great."

Before anything else could happen, I excused myself to go to the bathroom. "I'll be right back."

Friday night at George's was packed with people who were having the best time of their lives: people laughing, people clinking glasses, people feeding their children spaghetti. Everybody had dressed up, everybody looked happier than I felt, and as I walked uncertainly on my heels through the maze of tables—*hold your chin up, don't fall*—I thought, *Why not me? Why shouldn't I be happy like these people?*

Stepping into the bathroom was like being wrapped in somebody's grandmother's quilt. Too much pattern. Too much green. Dizzying. I leaned my back against the wall as I waited my turn.

Some lady who was washing her hands at the golden sink clocked me in the mirror and asked, "Are you okay?" She plucked a towel from the stack and dried her hands and looked at me with a concern that didn't seem to match the situation.

"I'm fine," I said.

"No one's in here, hon," she said, tossing the towel into the woven basket under the sink.

"Oh!" How embarrassing. But it was fine, because who was this lady? I would never see her again. And that's when I realized I'd never see anyone at this restaurant again. No one would know.

"You look like you're going to pass out," the lady said, her face tightening as she walked closer, her hand moving up in space like she was going to take my temperature with the back of her hand.

I blamed the dress—"this thing is so tight"—and pushed myself off the wall with slightly too much force. But, then again, that's what this situation called for. Force. Because people don't have the right to just touch you in public. People don't have the right to tell you what to do or who to be. All your choices are yours to make, and by making them, you prove to yourself that you aren't sleepwalking through your life, that you have the ability to reinvent yourself and the energy to surprise yourself, to take a left turn when everyone expects you to go right.

After the lady left, I looked at myself in the mirror.

Who are—

But I wasn't in the mood for deep questions.

———

Two glasses of champagne later, I felt sexy, and I knew exactly what I was doing, too. Two drinks melted you down just the right amount. More than that really wasn't necessary. I was proud of how I'd changed over the last six months. I had learned how to drink.

As the waves crashed below George's, I could feel them in my body. I looked at my phone on the table and wondered if Chris had written me back yet, but I didn't check. I didn't care. I was here with Brad.

"Chris says hi to you, by the way," I said, aware of how my mouth felt when it moved, and aware of how it appeared, too, because Brad was staring at it.

"Oh yeah?" he said. "You guys hanging out again, or what?"

"Not really." I tucked my hair behind my ear. "I don't know. We'll see."

I'd ordered a polenta mushroom dish, and Brad had ordered a pasta Bolognese. It was the most traditional thing he could have chosen. He twirled the pasta with his fork, using the spoon to help—so worldly—and told me about how the teenagers at his surf school were teaching him about resilience.

"There's this one kid, Joey, who just got hired at Starbucks, and he's so excited you'd think he'd won the lottery." And there was another kid named Stephanie, who'd started painting, and then there was Timmy, and there was Tommy—"not to be confused, they're very different"—and Kyle, who everybody called Buzz because she surfed like a bee.

As the night expanded into more night, my feelings for Brad brightened, and then they brightened more. Brad was honest, sensitive, kind. He was tan but not too tan. His eyes were like abalone. Abalone? Yeah, abalone. He told me he went to acupuncture once a week. He shopped at Whole Foods. He loved dogs. "But I'm not that into purse dogs," he said.

"I'm not into purse dogs either," I agreed, sipping the cognac we'd ordered for dessert.

On the drive home, I rolled down the window and held my face to the wind and felt like I was soaring. I was already imagining the kiss outside my front door.

But that's not what happened.

Brad pulled into the beach lot across the street from the house, turned up Van Morrison, and asked me to dance with him in the moonlight.

"Okay," I said, "but I have to take these heels off."

"Let me."

He slipped off my heels in a way that told me he understood touch in a way that he hadn't in high school. Then he pulled me up and twirled me around, and the sandy pavement itched the soles of my feet in the best way, and when he put his mouth on my neck, I was looking up at the moon, a crescent that hung like an earring, most of it dark, or waiting to be illuminated.

PART TWO

maybe

maybe

CHAPTER 32

stevie

I now had a secret.

And you know what? It felt good. I assumed that eventually, I'd tell Bonnie and Mom that I'd learned how to drink, and then we could all enjoy small amounts of wine together. Oh, and in this "eventually," I'd be dating Brad.

The morning routine didn't change at all. I wasn't hungover. I didn't feel sad. I felt great, actually—better than I had in a long time. When Bonnie asked me how the date had gone, that's what I said.

"It was great. I feel better than I have in a long time."

The person I really wanted to tell, though, was Chris, who still hadn't written me back.

If Everett's house had been a hipster brand of lipstick called Single Man's Junkyard during the first visit, then its new name was Possibly Contact Social Services.

The living room was in total disarray. Couch cushions

had been flung to the floor, and the magazines on the coffee table had been nudged to odd angles to make room for
the teetering stack of seven Domino's boxes in the center,
not that anyone was counting.

Bonnie dove in to hug Everett like she'd known him forever. "What happened?"

Everett, who'd clearly just woken up to open the door,
rubbed his eyes. "I went on a bender with gusto, like you
said."

"Way to get it all out, bro," Bonnie said. Then she told
him to take a shower and put on a real outfit that didn't in-
clude sweatpants. Everett, who had the body of a man but the
aura of a child, loped into the bathroom, sulky but grateful to
have been given specific directions about what to do next.

Once he'd closed the door, I turned to Bonnie and said,
"I feel like you have a crush on him."

"I know," Bonnie said. "And it makes no sense. He is *such*
a mess."

———

It's amazing how much some water can change a person's
entire outlook on life.

Everett emerged fifteen minutes later in a pair of Levi's
and a button-down shirt, his cheeks pink and alive, the
crusty nuggets in the corners of his eyes gone. He was almost sparkling, and Bonnie told him so. "*Now* you look like
a man who might find a nice lady."

I checked my watch to signal the turn we would be making, then said, "Let's get started," and corralled us toward
the room full of dirty clothes.

"Wait," Bonnie said. "We need a fan."

Everett framed his statement as a question. "I have one in a closet?"

Bonnie and Everett were giggling when they reappeared a minute later with the fan. Bonnie plugged it in. Everett turned it on. With the stream of air sort of diffusing the stench, I told Everett to pick up the first garment. He did. He was very obedient. It wouldn't have surprised me to learn that he'd been the number one student in his kindergarten class.

"Yes or no? You have five seconds."

Everett looked at the maroon V-neck from J.Crew in his hand, took a deep inhale, then stopped breathing.

"Yes?" Bonnie asked nicely. "Or no?"

"Maybe?"

"'Maybe' means 'no,'" I said.

"This was the second sweater Dagmar ever gave me."

It took Everett a literal ninety seconds to admit that maroon was probably not his favorite color, and it took him a literal fifteen seconds to place the maroon sweater he disliked in the bag that Bonnie was holding out for him.

"Bye," he whispered woefully.

It turned out that none of Everett's reasons for wanting to keep things were about him. They were about other people.

"Mom likes me in this one."

"Dagmar said this was my best belt."

Some of these other people didn't exist yet.

"What if my next girlfriend doesn't like dark denim?"

"Everett," I kept saying, my voice increasing in volume each time because I could see that authority was all he really wanted. "This is about *you*. You're creating the best version of yourself, and it is as this version that you will naturally attract a partner. Forget about your mom. Forget about your ex and your future girlfriend. What does *Everett* want?"

"Yeah," Bonnie rallied. "What does *Everett* want?"

It turned out that what Everett wanted was to dress more like a Seattle grad student than a thirty-eight-year-old orthodontist from Southern California.

In the end, he kept his beanies, his flannels, his graphic tees, and his button-down sweaters, but only the ones he'd bought in sizes that were technically too large for him. "That makes them grandpa sweaters," Bonnie said, "which fits with your Seattle vibe."

Like everyone else, Everett got stuck in a moment of fighting for the skinny jeans. "Maybe after I lose some weight?"

I said what I always did. "After you lose some weight, then you'll be a new person, and that new person can go out and buy himself some new jeans."

As far as belts, Everett owned forty-three of them, and they were all gifts from Dagmar. "Even though she bought them with my money," he revealed.

"What?" Bonnie was appalled. "How much money did you give to Dagmar while you were together?"

"Roughly fifty thousand dollars?" Everett said, and maybe it was hearing himself state the figure out loud that got him angry. "Fifty thousand dollars!" he yelled then, wrangling the mess of belts into the fresh Hefty Bonnie had just whipped open.

By the end of the clothing segment, Everett has discarded fourteen bags already, and this, I told him, was evidence of how he needed to stop letting other people tell him how to live and start trusting his own instincts.

"Trust your instincts, Ev-er-ett." Bonnie said his name was like it was a piece of candy in her mouth.

Next, we moved on to the kitchen, where Everett showed us several high-priced appliances still in their original packaging, including a Vitamix, a food processor, and an espresso machine.

"All from Mom. I've never used them," he said, clearly disappointed in himself, which I assumed was how his mother had trained him to feel when she didn't get her way.

I said, "Wow" and "How generous," and then asked Everett if he enjoyed cooking.

"I prefer takeout," he said. "Also, I'm not sure why Mom got me a food processor *and* a blender. Aren't they the same thing?"

"No," Bonnie said.

"Oh," Everett said. "Okay."

He decided to keep the espresso machine because he absolutely wanted to become a person who made espresso at home. Like the grandpa sweaters, this aligned with his inner identity as a Seattle grad student.

We set the machine up together. I didn't want an espresso, but Bonnie and Everett did. They each chose a flavor from the complimentary five-pack that came with the machine. Since he owned no espresso cups, they drank from the maroon IKEA mugs that Dagmar had picked out. Once they were done, Bonnie said, "Now let's get rid of these mugs. You hate maroon."

Everett smiled at her. "It's like you know me now."

Regarding the Vitamix and the food processor, Bonnie correctly pointed out if Everett had never even opened the boxes, then it might be best to donate those bad boys. "Some juice freak out there would give their pinky to own a Vitamix."

We all knew the reason for Everett's hesitation. Bonnie addressed it first. "Your mom will never know."

"Mom, I hope you don't find out about this," Everett said as he nudged the food processor and then the Vitamix across the counter toward Bonnie, who said, "You're like a lizard shedding its skin, dude."

The video games were all yeses, Everett said. "I don't need to go through them."

"Great," I said. "But they need to get off the floor and into some kind of shelving unit."

"I'll order one," Everett said, his chin up higher than before.

After that, we went through his books (mostly fantasy novels), the manuals for his electronic appliances (all trash, no argument ever), and then Bonnie slid open his closet door and pointed at a mysterious box. "What's that?"

Everett fiddled with his beanie. "Nothing."

The box, it turned out, contained all the letters that Dagmar had sent Everett from Croatia. We were surprised they'd dealt in actual paper after having met online. "I wanted to smell the paper and see her handwriting," Everett said. I thought that was understandable. Also sweet. I would have wanted the same things.

During their three blissful months of snail-mail correspondence, Everett and Dagmar had come to know each other through the expression of words—their own words and sometimes the words of others, because Everett frequently copied down poems and also some of his favorite quotes. "For example," he told us, "'We are made of starstuff.' That's Carl Sagan."

Why hadn't Everett become an astrophysicist like Carl Sagan, or a philosopher, perhaps one who strolled across the U Dub campus stroking his goatee, espresso in hand?

Of course, the answer wasn't hard to find. Her picture was on the fridge—as a magnet, because yes, she'd custom-ordered a magnet of her face and stuck it on her son's refrigerator. Earlier, while clearing the magazines off the coffee table, Everett had told us that his mom had chosen his profession for him. "Stability" was the full explanation.

Bonnie couldn't help herself. "Read us one of Dagmar's letters."

Everett complied, unfolding the pink stationery like it was still dear to him. "I love you, I love you, I miss you," he read. "She didn't know many English phrases."

"We are burning these," Bonnie said. "Right now."

Everett pressed the letter to his heart. "Really?"

Bonnie eyed the metal umbrella holder by the door. "In that thing."

Three minutes later, before any of us could change our minds, we were in the backyard, and Bonnie was striking a match. And with as much ambivalence as could be expected, given the fifty-thousand-dollar price tag of their relationship, not to mention its accompanying emotions, Everett crawled Dagmar's pink paper toward the fire, moving one hesitant degree closer to becoming the man he wanted to be.

Bonnie, a pro at fires—"Dwight loved camping"—dribbled the flame along the paper's edge as Everett looked on with the eerie, impenetrable gaze of a person you might choose to be in your cult if you were driving around in a white van scouting for new members.

Once the flames had eaten up all the ways in which Everett had been lying to himself, I said, "Now laundry."

It only took five minutes to teach Everett how to do his laundry. This is detergent. This is fabric softener. No, they are not the same thing. *HE* means *high-efficiency*. Don't overstuff the machines.

When we were done, Everett said, "Whoa, I've spent a lot of time avoiding a problem that's not even a real problem."

Bonnie told him to get that printed on a beanie, then took a ton of *After* pictures, plus a selfie of the three of us, and then we moved all his bags into the garage. Everett swore on his mother's life that he would call Habitat for Humanity in the morning. If his mother dropped by before then, Everett would keep her out of the garage. Easy. Except for that sometimes, she went into the garage without asking him first. She had a clicker.

Bonnie quickly solved this problem. "If she comes over, tell her you're a grown man now."

Everett absorbed this advice with feeling. "Mom, I'm a grown man now," he practiced.

"Exactly."

Bonnie dove in for a goodbye hug.

I shook Everett's hand.

He thanked us eleven thousand times.

On the drive home, Bonnie couldn't stop talking about how drastically Everett had changed in the last four hours. "I mean, *drastic*. I wonder how Dwight would be if he cleaned up his life. Dwight. Ugh." The "ugh" reverberated through the car as Bonnie looked out the window and said what I'd been waiting for her to say. "Decluttering seems dumb at first, but then you realize it's everything. Like, it's really *everything*."

"Bonnie, I have a question."

"What?"

"Are you ready for your Freedom Day?"

Bonnie didn't even try to decorate her answer.

"Yes."

CHAPTER 33

stevie

With the sun lowering in the sky, Bonnie and I went through her landfill while Mom switched between Instagramming and doing shoulder-opening exercises to counterbalance the effects of Instagramming on her body.

With her trademark certainty, Bonnie picked up her Hula-Hoop and said, "Goodbye." She tossed it to the side. With that same certainty, she decided to keep a pair of socks with avocados printed on them. "I love these." But with many items, like the old motorcycle gloves Dwight had bought her for Christmas last year, her certainty deserted her, and she stood there frozen, pulsing the item in her fist like she was testing what it what it would feel like to hold on and what it would feel like to let go.

"You have five seconds."

"I know, asshole."

At five—I was counting out loud—Bonnie uncurled her fist, letting the gloves flop onto the mound of rejects.

Bonnie was a fast worker. She was also a fast crier. She had a total breakdown after the gloves, and thirty seconds later she'd fully recuperated. Before we knew it, 75 percent of her old crap had been discarded, and she was hurling the last item at the pile—a book about beads—and shouting, "Done!"

I gave her puka-shell necklace the evil eye. "But *are* you?"

Bonnie, same as last time, responded to my hatred of her necklace with the story of its origins. "A wise man gave this to me in Hawaii."

I took us in an unexpected direction by asking, "What was his name?"

"Maha," Bonnie said at first, then corrected herself with, "or Mana," then admitted that she wasn't sure anymore. "It could have also been Horatio."

The name "Horatio" hung heavy in the air, and without me pushing any further, Bonnie made the silent admission that this necklace, like her memory of its entrance into her life, was a goner. Then she tried to take it off. But she couldn't undo the knot, and neither could I.

"I have scissors!" Mom called from the other side of the pool, and two seconds later she was cutting the thick hemp string herself, and then asking Bonnie where her poncho was. "I haven't seen it in a while."

Bonnie scrunched her face. "I hid it under the couch cushions."

"You put your nasty poncho in my couch?"

Ashamed, Bonnie went to fetch it. When she returned,

she said, "I want to cut a square piece and put it in my wallet."

Mom handed her the scissors. Bonnie cut an imperfect square, stuffed it into her pocket, and tossed the rest of the poncho at the pile. Then she called Goodwill and scheduled a pickup for the next morning.

CHAPTER 34

bonnie

At dinner that night, Stevie would not stop checking her phone. I knew she was looking for texts from Brad. So I just asked her, point-blank.

"Are you looking for texts from Brad?"

"Yeah," Stevie said. I thought she was trying too hard to sound nonchalant. "We're going over there in the morning, you know."

I said, "I know." Then I started going through all my regrets.

Hey, I have a proposition for you.

That's how it had started.

CHAPTER 35

stevie

There is something so real about a Sunday morning.

Because unlike the other days of the week, Sundays aren't designed for doing. They're designed for just being. They're when the everyday-ness of life is at its most brilliant, and so it shouldn't have been a surprise that on this Sunday morning, Brad opened his front door to reveal that he hadn't shaved. It wasn't bad. It was just real.

"Good morning," I said softly, aware that Bonnie was right behind me. Then I told him what I'd planned to say on the drive over. "We're all business today, okay?

"Word," Brad said.

"Oh, and I'd love to hang out again on Friday if you're free?" I put my hand on Brad's bicep because, I don't know, I just felt like that was what I was supposed to do.

For a second, he seemed worried. "I have to wait until Friday?"

I moved my face closer to his and whispered, "I need to take things slow."

Brad said he understood. "I just got out of something, so I should probably take it slow, too."

As we decluttered Brad's house, I realized why I'd let him get away. First, there were the terrible circumstances, which had clouded all my decisions back then. But really, it was because there was nothing wrong with Brad Rose. He was perfect. That was his problem. He was just perfect. And it had scared me. And I'd run away because I wasn't ready then. But now, maybe I was ready.

Brad was incredibly decisive. He knew exactly what he wanted and didn't want. He picked up the decorative wooden objects in his storage room with ease, even the heavy ones, and said yes or no to each one within three seconds. "I've been going through everything mentally for the last few days so I'd be ready," he said.

"Ass kiss," Bonnie said.

"Total ass kiss," Brad agreed.

This was the pattern of their banter for the two hours we were there: Bonnie jabbed Brad, and Brad remained immune to her jabbing.

Yes, no, yes, no, yes, no.

Without hesitation, Brad decided to donate about half of his trinkets. "If I need more, I'll just go on vacay again," he said.

We then moved into his bedroom to deal with the clothes. Along with some potentially worn-out board shorts, Brad had about two hundred T-shirts he'd gotten for free at surf competitions and stuff.

"I suggest keeping only the ones you've worn," I said, but I wasn't looking at Brad. I was looking at the mason jar of water on his bedside table again. Next to it was a small tub of Burt's Bees hand lotion and a book: *The Four-Hour Work Week* by Timothy Ferriss.

"I only wear the ones in the drawers," Brad said. "I've never even unfolded most of these other ones."

"Donate them all," Bonnie dared him. I could tell she wanted to leave.

"Stevie, what do you think?" Brad asked. I could tell he wanted to touch me.

"I agree."

While Bonnie bagged up the shirts, Brad asked me to decide on which board shorts he should keep. "You have better style than I do." Again, he was showing me that he was open to being molded. I liked that. Brad gave me power. Brad adored me. Brad thought I was amazing.

Most of his board shorts were too faded, or too hibiscus flower-y. I said no to all but two pairs.

Brad said, "You make my life better, Stevie Green."

Bonnie, in response to this, looked like she wanted to throw up, but said nothing.

I excused myself to use the bathroom, even though I didn't really need to use the bathroom. I just wanted to check my phone.

Before, I had thought, *She's busy*. But now I'd sent her multiple texts and she still hadn't responded? It was unlike her. Or at least unlike the *her* I understood her to be.

I asked myself if it would be a good idea to send her a text that said, *Are you avoiding me?*

And I decided that no, that was absolutely a bad idea, definitely the worst idea I'd had all day.

Then I rethought that.

You only live once?

So I wrote out the text.

Are you avoiding me?

And pressed Send.

Brad and Bonnie were gone when I came out of the bathroom. I followed the sound of their voices up the stairs, checking my phone on the way for Chris's response. I wasn't paying close attention. And I couldn't hear the words that they were saying, just a muffled rise and fall, the rhythm of an energetic conversation. They were talking fast until I got to the top of the staircase—and then they went totally silent.

They were looking at me.

I was looking at them.

The freezer rumbled with new ice cubes.

The obvious question seemed too needy, so I didn't ask it.

What were you guys talking about?

"We just came up here to get some water," Bonnie said. And it wasn't untrue. They both had mason jars of water in their hands.

Why did you stop talking when you saw me?

This also seemed too needy.

"So, after we leave," I said, "call Habitat for Humanity or Goodwill and schedule a pickup, okay?"

"Totes," Brad said.

"And have them take the pool table, too."

"Okay." Brad chuckled. "Anything else?"

I wanted to say *Yes, please buy some leather loafers today, and also please replace all your T-shirts with button-downs*, but I decided to be patient. We could do all of that later. Later, when I moved into this house, I could just throw his Vans away myself.

"Nothing else," I said.

Brad swung his powerful arms around me. "Text me later?"

I closed my eyes and kissed his lips. "Totes."

CHAPTER 36

stevie

The sun poured through the car windows as we drove, casting our lives in a lemony sheen. It was another perfect day in La Jolla, where the ocean and the breeze and the smell of eucalyptus constantly reminded you that life was beautiful and everything was fine and if you thought you had anything to complain about, well, then you were an asshole.

"What were you and Brad talking about in the kitchen?" I asked Bonnie. Because I didn't care if my sister thought I was needy. I only cared that Brad might.

She put her hand on the back of my neck and cooed, "How beautiful you look today."

"Shut up."

"Fine." Bonnie took her hand back. "I was telling him that he better treat you with *respect*."

I laughed. "What did he say?"

"That he would."

We drove on in silence for a while, and then Bonnie

said, "I've been thinking about telling Dwight I was cheating on him."

"Why would you do that?" I asked. "It would only hurt him."

"I know, and I don't want to hurt him," Bonnie said. "But if I don't tell him, then I'm a liar."

"But you've been lying for years."

"So I should just keep lying?"

"I mean, probably?"

"Okay, but what if the lie is eating me alive?"

We'd arrived at a stoplight. I checked my phone. Nothing.

"You know who'd be a great person to ask about this?" I asked, excited by the thought.

"Who?"

"Chris."

CHAPTER 37

bonnie

I didn't want to ask Chris, but Stevie wouldn't let it go.

"Just ask her. She's a therapist! It's like free therapy."

So I texted her.

Hey Chris, it's Bonnie. Can I ask you a question since you're a therapist? I've been holding on to a lie for a really long time. It's eating me alive. I want to be honest now, but I'm worried about hurting someone. What should I do?

"Perfect," Stevie said. "Tell me when she responds."

Stevie had barely finished that sentence when Chris wrote back, Oh my god, you did it.

Did I freeze?

Or was I melting?

My hands didn't shake as I deleted the text, which surprised me, because inside I was shaking.

Stevie was in her own little dreamworld, checking herself out in the rearview.

Then Chris wrote again.
Bonnie?
And again.
Hello?

CHAPTER 38

brad

I didn't think that Bonnie was going to say anything, but I wanted to be sure.

I made her promise.

"I won't!" she said.

It wasn't the best situation, but it wasn't the worst situation either.

I mean, right?

stevie

Life started to move fast. Probably too fast. Looking back, the moment it started moving fast was the exact moment I should have slowed down.

But I couldn't.

I needed to become La Jolla's number one decluttering guru. I felt like my real life couldn't start until that happened.

————

Between Monday and Friday, Bonnie and I decluttered four homes and had consultations with seven new clients. It was everything I'd ever wanted, to be so busy and productive, and throughout the week, I must have had the same thought at least fifty times: I couldn't be doing this alone. I shared this thought with Bonnie exactly once, on Wednesday night, when I was so exhausted that I wanted to cry for no reason. My comment moved Bonnie. "I feel so moved,

Stevie," she said, "and I would be totally depressed about Dwight if I didn't have this job right now."

So Bonnie needed me, too. We needed each other. We were the two sides of a roof, or the two wheels of a bicycle, working together to achieve the same goal. We carried out our morning routine like pros, never making excuses or trying to take shortcuts. Bonnie surfed while I ran to the pier and back. Then we showered and dressed and stood together in the Wonder Woman pose for two minutes, and I stared into my sister's eyes without looking away, and it wasn't even that awkward.

In the kitchen, she made her usual yogurt tower and curated our Instagram account while I worked on the "project" for thirty minutes. One day, she said that I had to start calling it a book or it was never going to become one. I thought that she was right. So after that, I said "book." But only to Bonnie and Mom. And I told them not to tell anyone.

At the end of every writing session, we took a selfie that included Wiener. Dogs, according to Bonnie, upped your likability by 30 percent.

Once we'd checked all our morning boxes, we spent the rest of the day driving around La Jolla from one mess to the next.

It wasn't until Friday night that I even thought about wine.

———

As Bonnie whipped open the first Hefty, Fancy the hair witch said, "What I really want to do is work at a salon."

"You have a bunch of money, dude," Bonnie said. "Just *build* a salon."

Fancy almost fell over. "Whoa. You're right."

The actual decluttering was almost unnecessary after that, because Fancy had received her big *aha*, but of course we still did it. And it was necessary. Who needs a couch with four blue cushions, one yellow cushion, and green armrest covers?

Nobody.

Fancy cried when we left. "I'll totally give you five stars," she said through her tears.

Oh yeah, this was the other thing. Bonnie had decided to just *tell* clients to please give us five stars. "We're trying to beat this chick Ursula in the polls." Her honest explanation hit a nerve, and people got on board quickly. I think it had something to do with Ursula's name. It was such a menacing name.

———

Veronica Wu was just as annoying the second time around.

"Will I ever be a size two again?"

This time I answered. "What do you think?"

Veronica grumbled and said she wanted to get rid of half—but only half—of her size twos. In the end, she said goodbye to two-thirds of them, then cried dramatically into a silk handkerchief with a frog embroidered on it. Her voice was snot-laden when she said, "Thank yoooou! And of course I'll give you a five!"

———

Stacy P had Googled "sustainable fashion" and wasn't interested. "Sorry."

I said that was fine. "You do whatever works for you."

Stacy P was just as dramatic as Veronica, but at least she eventually hoped to be paid for her talents.

"Yes!" she exclaimed over and over.

It was tiring, and also it hurt my ears. I didn't push her too much, except for when the garments were, as Bonnie put it, "busted beyond repair." Stacy P didn't fight. The F was so cheap that she knew all her discarded items could be easily replaced if needed. "I can buy it back."

In the end, her color-coded heaps decreased by about an inch each, and that was good enough for her. "I feel like a *winner*," she said, and stomped her foot once on the carpeted floor.

Was Stacy P a winner? The true answer was irrelevant. If she felt like a winner, then she could help us win by giving us five stars.

"Because we're trying to beat this chick Ursula in the polls," Bonnie said conspiratorially, like she was letting Stacy P in on a secret.

Stacy P said, "Girl, I got you." Then she took out her phone and gave us a five right there.

———

How did we have time to squeeze in seven new clients for consultations that week? I still have no idea. Bonnie summarized them again as lonely women with too much anxiety and a skewed perception of the universe—and she summarized the one man in the group, Henry, as a serial killer rodeo wrangler. He had a devilish leer and too much rope in his garage. I thought he was fine. He'd gone to Harvard. Plus, it wasn't like he was physically menacing. He was maybe five feet six on a good day and had very little muscle tone. If things got weird, I was sure we could outrun him.

"It's not a good system, though," Bonnie said. "We're going to these stranger's houses. Anything could happen. We need to start screening people. Let's do phone consultations from now on, dude. It will also save us a ton of time."

I felt like I'd been bonked over the head with a frying pan. "Oh."

Our follower count rose to 2,499. Multiple people requested that Wiener get his own account in our comments sections. Bonnie said she couldn't even deal with that right now.

Despite our new five-star reviews, the overall scores had not yet changed.

Us: 4.7.

Ursula: 4.8.

But soon, I knew that they would.

Two major things happened with Bonnie that week.

First, Dwight asked her to marry him. In a text. A text! She blocked his number.

And second, while explaining to me that the switch-and-replace was really the only true remedy for a breakup, she wrote this to Everett: Can I come play video games at your house sometime?

———

"I had a breakthrough today," Mom announced one night at dinner. "All my dolls are going to be sold as a pair from now on, and they're all going to be dead."

The two fairy dolls sitting on the table had the same long hair and sparkly clothes as before, but their faces were now skulls: upside-down hearts for the noses, black circles for the eyes, fish-bone smiles, bright flowers on each cheek. The tone was lightheartedly morose, kind of like Day of the Dead, but in drag.

"I'm calling them the dead dolls."

I thought that acknowledging death was a step in the right direction. And I tried to push Mom further in that direction.

"Do you want to spread our dead dad's ashes yet, Mom?"

"No."

"I think we should do it at his cliff," Bonnie said.

"*His* cliff," Mom repeated. "I've never heard you say that before."

———

Brad texted me all throughout the week.

How's today, gorgeous?

What's cooking, good looking?

Can't wait to see you on Friday!

It made me remember that he'd been like this in high school, too: predictable, loving, and a touch overbearing.

But then again, maybe he wasn't overbearing? Maybe I just wasn't good at accepting love?

In other words: maybe it was me, not him.

Chris hadn't written me back, and she hadn't written Bonnie back either. I knew that because I kept asking.

"Has Chris written you back yet?"

"Has Chris written you back yet?"

Bonnie kept saying no. At one point she said, "Why do you care so much?"

It was a good question that I wasn't sure how to answer, so I said, "I don't know."

I asked Mom what Chris's deal was. "I thought you said she wanted to be my friend."

"I'm sure she's just busy," Mom said. "I'll write to her right now."

On Friday night, we were all exhausted, but excited for our plans.

I was going out with Brad.

Bonnie was going to Everett's house to play video games.

And Mom was going to dinner with Donna again.

CHAPTER 40

stevie

For our date, I wore loose-fitting black pants and a cable-knit sweater. Brad wore jeans, a light blue button-down shirt, and loafers, just as I'd suggested. He'd texted me beforehand, asking me what he should wear.

Knock, knock, knock.

My life was a rom-com.

The casual speed at which I opened the door.

The sight of Brad, who I'd dressed in a text.

"You look dapper," I told him. He really did.

"You too." He laughed. "I mean, you look beautiful."

Our kiss, which was new and familiar all at once.

We drove to the same theater where we'd gone to see *Private Parts* starring Howard Stern when we were young.

"Remember?" he asked.

Yes, I remembered. I specifically remembered how, when the first shot of a naked woman appeared on the screen, Brad had covered my eyes for me. I didn't mention this to him now.

We went down memory lane after that. Remember how we used to call 411 instead of Googling stuff? Remember pagers? We thought we were so official with our pagers! Remember paging each other the numbers that spelled *BOOBLESS*? What were those numbers? Oh yeah, 80087355. And 143 was "I love you." Remember the Dippin' Dots kiosk at the mall? Remember how revolutionary Dippin' Dots seemed back then?

"I have this theory that if you take anything and make it tiny, people will buy it," I said. "People love tiny things."

Brad laughed. "So true."

His free hand was on my leg as he turned the wheel with the other, sliding us into a spot in the underground parking garage and then leaning over to kiss me before I expected him to. When he pulled away, he didn't pull away too far. He nuzzled my nose with his nose and locked his eyes on mine.

"Hi, Stevie Green."

"Hi, Brad Rose."

———

I'd forgotten that movie dates are kind of intense. Spending that much quiet time next to another person leaves a lot of room to make up stories based on minute details. I sat there wondering when Brad would open his Kit Kat bar and if he would do it with his teeth or his hands. He tried with his hands first, then resorted to teeth. Silently, he offered me a piece, and silently, I refused. I smiled as I shook my head so he wouldn't feel bad.

What happened in that movie? I know that Nicole Kidman was in it, with a lot of consternation on her pale face and her mouth slightly ajar. She was petrified, then bleeding, then running through a foggy wooded area where all the trees looked blue. Something bad was happening, and the source of the bad thing was a man, and the man owned a staggeringly ornate yacht and was revered in the community. In the company of others, the man was good. Alone, the man did shady things. He could not be trusted. He was a man who lived two lives.

After the movie, we dropped Brad's car at his house and walked to El Ranchero, where we ordered guacamole and two margaritas. It happened so fast. Brad asked me if I wanted one. I opened my mouth to say no, but "Yes" came out.

The mariachi band started a song and Brad smiled at me and I smiled back.

It's fine, I told myself.

It's fine, myself said back.

After the first margarita, it really was fine. I wasn't drunk. I was just the right amount of buzzed. Brad had some guacamole on his cheek, and I was happy to wipe it away for him. We discussed what he should put downstairs in place of the pool table. I had a bunch of great ideas, ideas I didn't even know existed within me.

After the second margarita, we started speaking in Spanish, and after the third margarita, or maybe it was the fourth, I lost count.

Then I lost time.

Later, I'd remember only flashes:

Stumbling down a dark street, a big leaf in my hand. A palm frond? Both of us doubled over, laughing hard.

The beach. Brad on top of me, his tongue deep in my throat. Cold, wet sand. Thinking, *The waves sound like foam*.

Brad's bed. His sheets, scratchy with sand. Him turning me over, tracing the curve of my scar, first with his fingers, then with his mouth, trying to be gentle while asking, "What happened to you, Stevie? What happened? What happened?"

CHAPTER 41

stevie

In the first moments of waking up, I was still dreaming.

I thought I might have been in Paris, and then I thought I might have been at home with Bonnie, and then I saw hair. Sandy blond hair. A man's hair. Brad's hair. And Brad's back, expanding and contracting as he breathed next to me in bed.

Fuck.

I wasn't wearing underwear.

Where was my phone?

My clothes were on the floor.

Fuck.

The tiny corner of the condom wrapper was almost imperceptible at first, and might have been invisible to anyone else, but I was looking for it. I was hoping so hard that it wouldn't be there.

Fuck.

This had happened before with many men, but it had never happened twice with the same man.

The drunk sex, the morning condom, and Brad, twenty years later.

I blinked at the ceiling. The rise and fall of Brad's breath became a ticking clock.

I had to leave.

I snuck out of bed and silently picked my clothes off the floor.

In the bathroom upstairs, I checked my phone.

At 11:40 p.m., Lex had texted me. Hey, can I take you out sometime?

Me: Ya!

Lex: Friday?

Me: Ya!

At 11:42 p.m., I'd texted Chris: xxxxx

She hadn't responded.

I remembered how once, when I was living in San Francisco, I opened a book and a note fell out.

Stop drinking, Stevie.

The handwriting was erratic. I'd been drunk when I wrote it.

So, *in vino veritas*?

My drunk self had a record of being smarter than my sober self. My drunk self knew that I was drinking too much long before my sober self was ready to fully receive that info. And now my drunk self apparently wanted to go out with Lex. And send Chris a bunch of *X*s.

But my drunk self also had a record of being much more stupid than my sober self. My drunk self had thought it was a good idea to rip a leaf off a plant and carry it down to a beach at night. My drunk self had decided to sleep with Brad.

I felt like two people, and I didn't know which person to trust.

In the mirror, I looked at my face long enough to know that I needed to wash it. I turned around and looked at the scar on my back through Brad's eyes.

Through Brad's eyes, it must have looked atrocious.

At some point, I'd have to answer his questions.

What happened to you, Stevie? What happened? What happened?

I carried out the next steps with no feeling. I dressed, I walked outside, I ordered a Lyft. I'd already started constructing the story I would soon be telling Mom and Bonnie about why I hadn't come home the night before, and by the time the Lyft arrived, I'd started to believe it myself. We made out, I slept over, it wasn't a big deal.

Because was it a big deal?

Maybe it wasn't.

I sent Brad a text: Left for work.

On the way past the street that led to the cliff that Bonnie had called *his* cliff, I reminded myself that I was only thirty-seven years old.

I was still young.

I had time.

CHAPTER 42

stevie

It scared me sometimes how good I was at lying.

"Oh, we made out and then fell asleep watching a movie," I said as Bonnie handed me a cup of coffee. It was 6:05 a.m.

"Didn't you *go* to the movies? And then you went back to his house and watched another movie?"

"Yup." I forced myself to laugh. "Double feature."

I drank the cup of coffee and three cups of water with Advil while Bonnie told me about her night with Everett. He'd worn a grandpa sweater and a beanie. They'd played a video game in which Bonnie had driven a yellow convertible that she now sort of wanted in real life. If it even existed in real life? Also, she told me, video games were freaking awesome! And yeah, they'd made out, too, and Everett was a *really* good kisser, like *really* good, like much better than Bonnie had expected. "It was almost like he became a different person when we kissed, dude."

I regret a lot of my life. That's what I was thinking as she told me about Everett.

But what I said was, "That's great, Bonnie. I'm so happy for you."

How to describe my routine that morning? It was hard, but I was telling myself it was easy. I'm not sure if lying to myself made it easier or harder, but it seemed like the only option at the time.

I ran faster than I wanted to. Again, I imagined I was running away from something. A shark. A fanged bear. A fanged albatross. The wind hurt my face. My brain was a yolk sloshing around inside an egg.

I told myself I was fine.

Stevie, you're fine.

I looked at the ocean. The ocean seemed fine. Actually, it seemed so majestic that I wanted to cry.

So I made myself run faster.

By the time I got home, I'd decided that there was no way I would go out with Lex. She was too young and she had too many lines on her face. But then in the shower, I reconsidered, for two reasons:

First, if I was going to end up with Brad, then I needed to make sure that I didn't like women.

Second, if I went out with Lex, then I could tell Chris that I was going out with Lex and we could bond over what it was like to date women. And she could give me pointers? And I could prove to her and to myself that I was open-minded. Really, I would have loved to be one of those people who said, *I'm fluid*, because just in terms of simple math, those people had the best chance of finding a partner.

Gender is not important to me. I'm fluid.

Maybe everyone wants to be able to say this? It's not only statistically intelligent. It also just sounds so next-level.

After having gone through my reasons and formally deciding that, yes, I would go out with Lex, it was time to text Chris. I got out of the shower with a sense of urgency, wiped my hands on the towel, and picked up my phone.

Hi! Sorry, I think I butt-texted you last night. Can we please get together? I agreed to go out on a date with a woman and I'm nervous.

Did I recognize that this was manipulative?

I did, but at this point, many days into being ignored by Chris, I was willing to say whatever I needed to say to get what I wanted, which was apparently her attention.

———

Just as Bonnie rang Polly Johnson's doorbell, Chris texted me back.

Hike tomorrow?

I was grinning as Polly opened the door.

The first thing she said?

"I swear I know you girls from somewhere, but I still can't figure out where."

"Maybe the grocery store or something?" Bonnie said.

Like the last time, we came to no conclusions.

For the next six hours at Polly's totally depressing house, I not only kept it together. I put on a great show. I was a professional businessperson with an unflinchingly chirpy attitude. The best way to combat a dark atmosphere is with sparky energy. Also, I was probably kind of high off Chris's text, so keeping a smile on my face wasn't that hard.

Polly spent most of the six hours talking about Ed. Once, Ed had gone down to Rosarito to buy some terra-cotta wall hangings and he ended up buying a man a car! Another time, back when Ed was still poor, before he'd taken the bar exam, he'd bought meals for an entire family at Denny's. "Even when he had close to nothing, he was still giving it away," she told us.

We listened attentively and looked adoringly at pictures of Ed in a way that said, *We care*.

Then we advised Polly to get rid of most of Ed's things.

Begrudgingly, she agreed.

But it took forever. About every item, Polly needed to share the story about how it related to Ed. "He bought this lamp one day when he was feeling under the weather and . . ."

Between comments about Ed, she made comments about us. "How long has your hair been short?" she asked. "You touch it as if it's new." About the way Bonnie looked at her phone, she said, "Romance." And of course Bonnie then told her about Everett and the text he'd just sent about wanting to meet her dog. Polly already knew about Wiener because she'd seen him on Instagram. It turned out that Polly had seen a lot on Instagram. "I'm online a lot. It's where I get answers."

I don't know why that surprised me, because it made absolute sense. What was the perfect outlet for both Polly's depression and her hawkishness?

The Internet.

What Polly had failed to show us during the consultation, "because I didn't want you to make me feel bad about it," was her office. "I call it my cave," she said. Her cave was downstairs, next to the garage, and if I'd stumbled upon it without knowing who it belonged to, I would have assumed the owner was either a private investigator or a conspiracy theorist.

On the walls she had pinned aging newspaper articles about various happenings in La Jolla. Apart from being all being local, they seemed to have no theme. On her crappy old desk, which was chipping at the corners, were stacks of more articles. And recipes. 20-Minute Leek and Potato Soup. Multiple mugs and water glasses and half-eaten bags of chips were evidence that Polly spent most of her time down here, sitting in her cracked leather chair, which was the same as Ed's upstairs.

"You need to get rid of this," Bonnie said. "It's like the other one. Broken."

"It's not broken."

"Polly, it's tilting at an angle. So it's broken."

Polly pursed her lips. "Fine."

"What's with all these articles?" I asked.

"I like information," Polly said. "Don't you want to know who your neighbors are?" She moved to the filing cabinets against the wall. They were ancient and metal and probably weighed thousands of pounds each. "And I *do* have an organizational system"—she opened a drawer—"which I think you would appreciate."

Polly kept the drawer open long enough for me to read a few labels:

LJ KIDNAPPINGS

LJ VIOLENT CRIMES

LJ EMBEZZLEMENT

Then, as if suddenly feeling too exposed, she slammed the drawer shut and crossed her arms over her chest and said, "Never mind, I don't want to show you this."

"You're like a historian," Bonnie said.

"Librarian," Polly said, "before I retired. Let's go back upstairs."

We went back upstairs.

Or at least we started to, until Polly said, "Wait!"

We paused on the staircase.

Polly flew back into her cave.

Seconds passed. Then more seconds. It was enough seconds for me to call, "Polly?"

"I figured it out!" she called back.

And she emerged from her cave with a newspaper clipping in her hand.

"*This* is how I know you!"

LA JOLLA MAN WITH CANCER COMMITS SUICIDE

Just underneath the headline was a picture of our father.

He looked ridiculously happy.

CHAPTER 43

stevie

So here's the last major thing I haven't told you about yet.

My dead dad.

I still don't enjoy talking about this.

My dead dad's name was Jack Green. From what I can gather, Jack Green was a loser. Yes, he was charismatic, and yes, he was smart, but he accomplished nothing substantial during his lifetime. He never got a real job. Instead, he found rich women to take care of him. My mom was the last one. He was one of those guys who drove around the tiny dot of La Jolla like it was the whole world. The tennis courts. The beach. Drinks at the Marine Room. Back home for more drinks.

"He made a mean piña colada," Mom told us once.

In the early days, they drove all over San Diego trying to find the best piña colada. They drove to Mexico, too. Never in this story was the verdict presented, because it wasn't a story about piña coladas. It was a story about a search, and a story about a courtship.

They got married one year in. Soon after that, they bought the house on Moonridge. And soon after that, they had me. By that time, Dad's drinking had become a problem. Mom asked him to stop. But he couldn't. She threw his beer in the trash. He bought more. He liked to drink during the day while gardening.

Not long after Bonnie was born, he started complaining about a pain in his stomach. He went to the doctor. Stage-four liver cancer was the diagnosis. For one or two weeks, he was determined to fight. He quit drinking. Mom thought there might be hope.

She was wrong.

One day, Dad went to the Marine Room, got wasted, and drove himself to a cul-de-sac off Torrey Pines Road that sits right on a cliff. The view from this spot is magnificent, and Dad used to go there a lot to think. Or to drink. Or both. This is what Bonnie called *his* cliff. This is where I went after I found those flyers. This is where I've spent zillions of hours of my life asking the same questions.

What was he thinking the moment right after he jumped?

What was he thinking as he started to fall?

Was he regretting it already?

CHAPTER 44

stevie

Bonnie cried all the way home from Polly's house. "I miss him so much!"

I didn't cry. How can you miss someone you had never really known?

When we told Mom about the article, she started crying, too. "Oh my god, I remember when that came out."

Nobody felt like ordering dinner. Bonnie took a bath. I ate some cashews and got into bed early. Mom came into my bedroom and told me she was proud of me for changing my life and making healthier choices and not becoming my father. "For a while there, I was worried. But now I know you're going to be okay."

Stumbling down a dark street, a big leaf in my hand.

The beach. *The waves sound like foam.*

Brad's sandy sheets.

The condom wrapper.

What happened to you, Stevie?

I felt like a fraud. I still had those wine bottles in the car and the sour taste of margarita deep in my throat as I said, "I'm *already* okay, Mom. Don't worry."

In the low light cast by the one small lamp in my room, Mom looked more fragile than usual. She set her hand on her cheek. Her eyes were bloodshot from crying. Her ponytail had come loose, and for some reason the way it drooped made me unbearably sad. I thought about how hard it was to be a parent, and about how I'd never really sacrificed anything for anyone before.

After she left my room, I turned off the light and checked my phone. Brad had written me a long message about how he felt everything was meant to be, you know? But next time, we should probably do that when we've had less margs? Ha. Also, he loved my new hair. He couldn't remember if he'd told me that yet or not. Anyway, he wanted to see me again. Soon? And: Do you like ceviche?

Meanwhile, Lex had sent me the name and address of a restaurant in PB. Friday okay?

I sighed.

Who was I, and what did I want?

I was a woman with a headache and a plan. I'd go out with Lex just to make sure I didn't like her, and then I'd see Brad again, and we wouldn't drink, because I was done drinking forever, and then time would pass and things would happen and the end of the story was that I would fall in love with him. That's what I was thinking as I responded to Chris.

Since I now understood her to be a person who might not respond, and since there's nothing more alluring than someone who doesn't respond, I spent extra care crafting my message.

Torrey Pines? 2pm?

It took me five minutes to land on this.

You know that feeling you get when somebody you've been waiting to hear from texts you? You see their name on the screen and your heart shifts inside your chest and it feels like drugs?

That's how I felt when Chris wrote me back.

Sure.

PART THREE

oh

stevie

There are lots of things to get high on, and the best one is exercise.

My run that morning was borderline spiritual. I was swept up in my music, lost in the rhythm of my feet hitting the sand. It was like I had no body. It was like a trance. The ocean seemed bluer, the seagulls seemed perkier, and the sky seemed much more expansive than usual.

I was already imagining how I would describe this later to Chris. *I had an* awesome *run. And then an* awesome *decluttering for this guy Henry, who weirdly had a ton of rope in his garage, but we got rid of all of it.*

Also: *Yeah, we're only one tenth of a point away from Ursula, so I'm hoping that within the next month or two, we'll be number one.*

And: *No, I haven't thought about the high school thing at all! Why are you even bringing that up?*

By the time I had showered and dressed, I'd gone over my side of this imaginary conversation multiple times. I knew how I would feel, I knew how she would react, I had the future all planned out.

Then Bonnie, from across the house, screamed.

She sounded like a hyena.

"Stevie!"

She bounded into my bedroom with her phone.

"You are not going to believe this."

"What?"

"We're *tied*!"

My first thought: *I get to tell Chris that we're* tied *now.*

CHAPTER 46

chris

The cliffs from afar looked like a candy bar that someone had bitten into. Caramel, scraped by teeth. The sun was bright, almost blinding. A lizard skittered across the dirt so fast that I thought I might have imagined it.

Honestly, I felt crazy.

This was something I was always suggesting that my clients not say.

Is it helpful to call yourself "crazy"?

The question gave most of them pause, and then they'd say that no, it probably wasn't that helpful. But one guy last week, Leon, had said, "You're not listening. I feel *crazy*."

His wife had just left him.

Stevie had never, to my knowledge, mentioned the possibility of dating a woman. So when I got her text, I was more than surprised. I was startled. My ears buzzed. A lightness filled my head. After the shock, I was flooded with hope, so much hope that it scared me. I knew that the difference between drowning and floating peacefully underwater was slim. I knew that I couldn't stop the flood of hope, but I tried anyway.

Don't get your hopes up, Chris. Keep your hopes small and unseen.

My plan was to go into therapy mode. I would listen to what she had to say and be supportive. My heart had different plans, though, and also a bunch of questions, which really all boiled down to one question: *Will Stevie Green fall in love with me now?*

I thought, too, about what would happen if she did. I'd put her on a pedestal for all these years. I'd given her special powers. But maybe our real life together wouldn't be that great. She'd only just stopped drinking. She wasn't going to meetings. She had never, to my knowledge, had a girlfriend. If somebody had told me these facts about any other woman, I would have said, *No thanks.* But it was Stevie, and there was just something about Stevie. The way I felt around her was a way I'd never felt around anyone. It was simple. It was just like, *Oh, you're the one.*

My other plan for our hike was to dig for information. I didn't really think that Bonnie was responsible for the flyers—I still thought it was Brad—but why hadn't she written me back? And why hadn't Kit returned my calls? I'd left several messages.

Part of me wanted to let the drama of high school go, but part of me didn't. It sucks to get blamed for something you didn't do. Also, if Stevie thought I had betrayed her, then how was she going to fall in love with me?

Don't be nervous. Be yourself.

This is what I was thinking as I waved to Stevie, who'd just pulled her car into the spot right next to mine.

CHAPTER 47

stevie

Even her wave was self-assured. There was no desperate flapping, just the calm lift of a single hand. It almost looked like she was taking an oath.

Do you swear to tell the whole truth and nothing but the truth?

"Hey!" I called, and immediately, I thought I sounded too desperate. This is what happens when people avoid you. You become desperate around them. When people give you less, you want more. It's simple supply-and-demand theory. The funny part about it is how the wanting takes over the facts. Because who was Chris to me? Was she my friend? Was she my enemy? I wasn't sure anymore.

Do not talk about high school, Stevie.

Honestly, I was hoping that by pretending to *not* want what I wanted, I would get it: a confession.

"Hey, Stevie," Chris said, and gave me a loose hug. "Sorry it took me so long to get back to you."

"Oh, no worries," I said. "I've been super busy with work."

The trail was carved up by dried rivulets and snake holes, so I kept my eyes on my feet as I told Chris about the Henry job we'd finished earlier. "An *obscene* amount of rope, but we got rid of all of it." I'd thought to add the word "obscene" on the drive over. Chris laughed, but not very hard. "That's great."

"And this morning? I had an *awesome* run. I mean, I just love running so much. And then I came home and found out that we are *tied*!"

"Amazing," Chris said. "Tied with who?"

Why had I assumed that Chris would know what I was talking about?

"Ursula de Santis. She's the number one—"

"Oh, wait, sorry," Chris said. "I think your mom mentioned this."

"Within a month or so, I think we'll be winning," I said.

"Wow," Chris said, but she didn't seem that interested.

We were coming up on the skinnier part of the trail, and I slowed my pace so that she'd go ahead of me. I wanted to watch her rather than be watched by her. What I saw: her red shoes, her black leggings, her striped T-shirt, the olive skin of her neck, the precise line where her dark brown hair stopped, and her hat, which was the color of sage.

"So, tell me about this date with a woman," she said matter-of-factly.

I kept my tone even, upbeat. I poked fun at myself without being self-deprecating. I laughed when it seemed natural. Basically, I imagined what a totally confident woman in my situation would do, and then I did that.

"Her name is Lex. She's the friend of a client. She asked

for my number, and I thought she was going to call to set up a consultation, but then she asked me out." I laughed here. "Which I guess means that she assumed I date women?"

Chris didn't answer. I thought I saw her nod, but I wasn't sure.

"Anyway, I'm just . . . I guess I just wanted to ask you . . . how you knew . . . or, like, when you knew?"

Chris stopped. She turned around. I was glad I was wearing sunglasses so she couldn't see my eyes.

"I knew when we kissed in seventh grade, dude. In a *closet*!" Chris laughed. "Which was your idea, by the way."

"It was?"

I already knew it was.

"Yeah, it was." Chris started walking again.

"Okay, but you didn't come out in seventh grade," I said.

"Hell no. It was the nineties. There were no gay kids at Muirlands. Also, I wasn't really sure I was gay either."

"But you just said you were."

"I guess it's more like in retrospect, that's when I knew. But I wasn't clear until high school."

I flashed back to Chris at eighteen. She was wearing overalls, and she was crying in my car. "I don't want to be your friend. I want to be your *girl*friend!" I couldn't remember what I said back, but I knew it wasn't very nice. This was when we'd stopped talking. This was exactly five days before the morning of the flyers.

I cleared my throat. "I'm sure I said this at the time, but I'm really sorry if I hurt you."

"No, you didn't say that at the time, Stevie," Chris said with a definite edge, and this edge was like an earthquake. It shook me, and it shook all the pieces up, too. Suddenly I felt like I'd misunderstood the puzzle.

"Oh. Well, I'm sorry," I said lamely. "I'm really sorry."

As we walked on in silence, I was thinking, *Oh my god, for the last twenty years I've been wanting an apology from Chris. And for the last twenty years Chris has been wanting an apology from me.*

And then Chris said the same words I'd said to her at the Pannikin. "I forgive you."

I heard myself say, "Thanks."

The trail steepened, and then it steepened more, and then there was the final jump from the rocks onto the beach. The waves lapped. The bunches of kelp looked like chunks of hair on the floor of a salon. When a middle-aged couple walked by us and said, "Hi," I wondered who they thought Chris and I were to each other.

"Do you want to go back up the way we came or do the loop?" Chris asked with her hands on her waist like she was ready for anything.

I craned my neck and looked up at the trail, which seemed even steeper from down below. *I hate hills,* I thought. *I hate San Francisco.* "I hate backtracking," I said.

Chris laughed.

"What?"

"Nothing," Chris said, walking away from me already. "Let's do the loop."

We took off our shoes and trudged north on the sand toward Del Mar. For a while we reminisced about fonder memories while avoiding the bad ones. There was the summer we were obsessed with our bicycles, and the time we thought it was a good idea to eat ants for protein, and the fun of jumping from the trampoline into the pool in her backyard. And then there was the first time we ever spoke, in sixth grade, when Chris asked me if she could use my pencil sharpener because I looked like a responsible girl who might have one.

"Yeah, and remember pagers?" I said. "Brad and I were just talking about that."

"You and Brad are still talking," Chris said. She seemed surprised.

"We've gone out a few times."

"And now you're wondering if you're into women."

"I didn't say that."

"You didn't?"

"Not exactly."

"Listen," Chris said. "It's all good. After I stopped drinking, it took me two years to realize that I hate vanilla ice cream."

What I felt like she was telling me: *You don't know who you are.*

We were in the lower parking lot now, putting our shoes back on. Chris was faster than me because she hadn't untied her laces.

"Also, I think it's great to date more than one person at the same time," she said. "It helps you compare. I told your mom the same thing."

"My *mom*?"

"Yeah, we signed up for Hinge together. She didn't tell you?"

"What!"

"Oh no," Chris said. "Maybe I shouldn't have said that."

I set my eyes on the horizon then. Maybe it was a natural reflex, an attempt to feel like I knew where I was in space. Chris was on a dating app? *Mom* was on a dating app? The horizon didn't look like a straight line. It seemed to be slanting.

I finished tying my shoe. Chris offered me a hand and pulled me up, and when she did that, I remembered how strong she was. We started up the winding road back to our cars, and I noticed that our feet were hitting the pavement at the same time. Right, left, right, left. For a little while, I didn't speak, and neither did Chris, and somehow, the silence between us was comforting. It felt like something we'd both agreed to without speaking.

Eventually, Chris said, "Will you ask your mom to call me back, by the way? I've left her a few messages."

I remembered Mom saying, "I'll write to Chris right now." Had she never done that?

"Sure," I said.

"And tell Bonnie I'm still happy to help her with her problem if she wants."

"Bonnie said you never responded to her text."

Chris didn't slow her pace. "I *did* respond."

CHAPTER 48

stevie

The second I drove out of that parking lot, I called Bonnie.

"Why did you tell me Chris never responded to you?"

"Oh," Bonnie said. "Did she? Let me check." After a moment: "Oh yeah, I guess she did. I must have missed it."

I called Mom, who said she'd been meaning to get in touch with Chris, but she'd been so busy she kept forgetting.

"Are you on a dating app?"

"I was," Mom said, "but I deleted it."

When I got back to the Shores, I reached into the pocket behind my seat. I was going to throw the wine out, because suddenly, I sort of wanted to drink the wine. But the bottles weren't there. Had Bonnie found them again? She must have. There was no other reasonable explanation. I thought it was strange that she hadn't mentioned it to me.

I thought it was strange that Mom hadn't mentioned dating.

I thought it was strange that Chris had laughed when I'd said, "I hate backtracking."

If there was a day when I tuned into the fact that I wasn't the only one living a secret life, then this was that day. Everybody was lying. But I guess I assumed the lies were all little and white, like my wine lie, and like the future lie I planned to tell Mom and Bonnie about what I was doing on Friday night, when I went out with Lex. And so I thought it was fair. It almost made me feel better. If everybody else was lying, then my lies seemed less devious.

Who, at this point, did I think had betrayed me in high school?

Honestly, I still thought it was Chris. And now, after seeing her, I was starting to understand why. I'd hurt her. She'd made a rash decision. If I were her, I probably wouldn't have confessed either.

CHAPTER 49

stevie

The next morning, as Bonnie and I walked home from the beach, I was thinking about how the light in Southern California is whiter than in other places I've lived. It's hollow rather than buttery. It's the color of one egg mixed with three egg whites. I imagined saying this to Chris. Then I realized it would be a good idea to test it out on Bonnie first. But she was talking.

"Everett was telling me about this one chick's teeth, and oh my—"

"Bonnie?"

"Yeah."

"Don't you think the light in San Diego kind of looks like one egg mixed with three egg whites?"

"Ha," Bonnie said.

I thought it was a positive enough reaction.

On the mat outside our front door were flowers wrapped in that familiar parchment paper.

"Flowers!" Bonnie said. "I bet they're from Everett."

I already knew they were from Brad, and I was right.
Roses this time, and red ones. I picked them up and read the
note.

Can't wait to see you on Saturday!

"He's pining, dude," Bonnie said.

A few days earlier, I'd told Brad that I could have lunch
with him on Saturday. Mom had convinced me that we
needed to take a day off. "If you don't recharge," she'd said,
"you're going to burn out." It was probably only because she
presented me with an article about burnout that I agreed.
Apparently, burnout was a syndrome now. I hadn't known
that.

I'd asked Brad to have lunch and not dinner because we
needed to back things up. I didn't want him to think I'd be
spending the night again, and I didn't want to get wasted at a
restaurant again. For good measure, I'd told him that I was
on a cleanse. So I can't drink. ☺

His response?

Oh sweet, can I be on a cleanse with you? ☺

I wrote, Of course!

But what I had meant by *Of course* was *I suddenly feel a
gnawing sense of uncertainty about everything, and I'm hoping it
will go away soon.*

CHAPTER 50

bonnie

Our client that morning was an anxious housewife named Trudy who'd just moved here from Ohio, and you know what? She was great. I told her to get rid of a bunch of stuff that was obviously trash, even though, yes, I knew she'd just had it shipped from Ohio. Stevie followed up with, "It's time to start your new life here now, with new things."

But Trudy isn't who I really want to talk about.

Who I really want to talk about is Chris Dane.

Stevie and I were kicking ass now. We had our routine down. I felt like we'd never been closer. Honestly, the closer we got, the less I wanted to tell her about high school. But the longer I didn't tell her about high school, the worse I felt. It was like exploding from two sides, if that even makes sense. I didn't know what to do, so I did nothing.

Or, I wanted to do nothing, but Chris Dane would not leave me alone. She'd texted me seven hundred times.

Bonnie?

Why won't you answer?

Can we please talk?

I planned to keep delaying, but then while we were at Trudy's house, she wrote, Bonnie, if you don't respond, I'm going to call Stevie right now and tell her you did it.

That scared me enough to write back. Don't!

This was right after Stevie had thrown her arm around me and said to Trudy, "We used to be enemies, but now we're best friends." Her arm was still around me when I read Chris's response.

We need to meet this weekend. And you're bringing your mom.

CHAPTER 51

stevie

I was in a good mood before lunch, and then something crazy happened. When I thought about it later, though, I realized that the truly crazy thing was that it hadn't happened earlier.

We ran into Ursula.

It started out passively enough. The marine layer was just burning off, and the sun was peeking through the blanket of fog like a promise you hope will be kept. Bonnie braided her arm around mine as we moved toward the minimal foliage of Girard Gourmet's small outdoor seating area. We took our place in line and quietly admired the heaps of cookies displayed in the window. There were the usual suspects: the surfboard-shaped cookie that said LA JOLLA against a beach background, the orange garibaldi fish, the smiling yellow suns; and today's guest stars: red crabs, blue whales, brown dogs. These cookies were part of the inheritance of anyone who'd grown up in La Jolla, and Bonnie and I must have been too caught up in nostalgia to notice Ursula at first, even though she was standing right in front of us in line. Neither of us had ever met her, and we couldn't see her face, so I guess it was understandable that we didn't recognize her immediately.

When I clocked her white hair, I did think that it seemed strangely familiar. And her body, too, seemed like one I'd seen before. It was the shape of a Russian doll, tiny and tubby and wearing the attire of your basic old person: polyester slacks, a cashmere cardigan, and on her feet, a pair of witchy black loafers with square toes.

Still, I wasn't sure that it was Ursula. It could have been a lot of people.

But then she turned so I could see her face in profile, and yes, oh my god, it was her!

When you have an archenemy you've only ever seen online, it feels very strange to encounter them in real life. I felt bigger and smaller at the same time. I started sweating. I wrapped my hand around Bonnie's arm and squeezed, then leaned in to whisper, "Ursula."

Bonnie registered the news with a sharp inhale.

Then she did the opposite of what I'd planned to do, which was to remain silent.

"Ursula?"

The way Ursula whipped around made me think that my story about her as a drug user might have been correct. She had the energy of a person who could set off a microwave just by walking past it. Even before she'd spoken, it was clear why she was so successful. I no longer felt bigger and smaller at the same time. I just felt smaller. This made no sense because Ursula was probably four feet eleven on a good day, but oh my god, she had *presence*. And it was terrifying.

"Yes?" Ursula said. "Who are you?" Her eyes were like hard black coals.

"I'm Stevie." I stuck out my hand, which Ursula shook with the tenacity of a blender.

"And I'm Bonnie. Bonnie Green."

"We're the Clean Green Sisters."

"Aaaah." Ursula's mouth opened, which made her seem kind of vulnerable. I was almost tricked into thinking she was going to be nice.

"I so appreciate your work," I said.

This was total bullshit and Ursula called me on it. "No, you don't."

"How old are you?" Bonnie asked.

Ursula's eyes shot open. *"Rude."*

Here, our dramatic conversation paused because it was Ursula's turn to order. "Turkey sandwich, extra avocado, lemon pepper. Thank you, Billy."

It irritated me beyond reason that Ursula knew the name of the guy who worked at Girard Gourmet and I did not, and he seemed to like her, too. "Great choice, Ursula," he said with a wink.

Then Ursula gave us her full attention. This was what she said:

"Do you girls know that I built my business from the ground up? Nobody thought I would succeed. As a child in Dallas, I was told I would be a loser forever. And look at me now." She did a Vanna White hand move around her own face, as if she herself was the prize. "So. If you think for one second that I am going to let some young whores tear me down, then you are wrong."

"Oh my god, did you just call us *young whores*?"

Bonnie thought it was funny. My T-shirt was damp with sweat.

"This has happened occasionally over the years." Ursula now seemed bored. "A new act comes to town. They think they can become popular. Then I demolish them and they go back to being housewives. Or real estate agents."

"You're not going to demolish us," Bonnie said matter-of-factly.

Ursula laughed. "Have you checked Organizely in the last hour? I have twenty new reviews and four-point-nine stars now."

"How is that possible?"

"I asked my old clients to review me."

"That's not fair!" Bonnie said.

"Of course it's fair," Ursula said. "They're *my* clients."

Billy handed Ursula her sandwich. "Thank you, Billy, you're the best," she said sweetly.

She turned to us, hissed the word, "*Demolish*."

And then she speed-walked out the door.

stevie

Life continued to move too fast, and I continued to think, *You should probably slow down*, but I couldn't. It felt like everything was converging. It felt like the walls were closing in. It felt like I was in a tunnel and a flood was coming to thrust me out onto the edge of a waterfall, and then I would be falling, and either the end was going to somehow work out beautifully or I was going to die on impact.

The sense of impending doom was about many things, but most tangibly, it was about Ursula de Santis and her unforeseen resurrection. Getting old clients to review her was such a cunning move, and I had to admit that I respected her ruthlessness. I might have even respected her cruelty, or at least it gave me pause.

Did you have to be a bitch to succeed as a woman in this world?

Would it be in my best interest to become a meaner person?

I wasn't sure yet. All I knew was that we had to keep

going, and now we had to keep going without the shine of hope, because the future seemed dismal. How many old clients did Ursula have? I suspected thousands.

———————

From Tuesday to Friday, we decluttered the homes of six new clients and did a dozen consultations over the phone. Bonnie did half of those. I did the other half.

In the car, driving from one client to the next, we listened to *How I Built This with Guy Raz*, a podcast about redemption stories in business. Three-fourths of the way through every episode, the business owner being interviewed seemed destined to fail, but then at the very last second, like one split second before they were about to give up, they shot to the top and became rich, powerful, and famous all at once.

On the one hand, I thought these were all fluke stories.

On the other hand, I ate them up like I was starving.

———————

Bonnie kept telling people to give us five stars because we were trying to beat Ursula, and now, after our encounter at Girard Gourmet, she was dishing out details.

"We ran into her, and she is *horrible*. Like a cross between a Stepford wife and a rat."

Was this classy?

Did I care?

Nope.

All I cared about was getting five stars.

———————

Over the course of the week, I started to notice things I didn't want to notice.

A bottle of scotch on a desk.

A dented Corona Light can in a recycling bin.

A jumbled liquor cabinet that seemed like an afterthought to its owner did not seem like an afterthought to me. It seemed to be whispering, *Hello?*

It wasn't hard to squash the whispering, however. All I had to do was remember waking up in Brad's bed.

Never again, I whispered back, but internally, of course. It's not like I was insane.

I'd planned not to tell Bonnie about how Mom and Chris had signed up for Hinge together because I didn't really want to talk about Chris, but apparently I couldn't help myself.

"Are you *serious*?" Bonnie said. "We've been begging her to start dating for *years*, and *Chris* is the one who finally convinced her?"

That night, Bonnie brought it up at dinner.

"I can't believe you're dating and you didn't tell us, Mom!"

Mom repeated what she'd told me earlier. "I deleted the app." Then she revealed new information. "But somebody wrote to me on Instagram."

His name was Bruce Dover. He was a sculptor. He lived in Del Mar. And he'd written Mom to say that he loved her new work. So now they were chatting.

But at this point, Mom was more interested in Instagram than she was in Bruce. She'd read all these articles about the harms of social media and decided that, yes, for young people it was very harmful. "But for older people, it's a great way to feel young again."

Mom was posting at least three pics a day and making tons of new dead dolls. "I think that knowing I can show them off right when I'm done makes me work faster."

She had eight hundred followers already, and this fact was unbelievable to her.

"Eight *hundred*," she said, kind of dazed.

We got five stars for every job we did that week.

Ursula got twenty-five new reviews, and they were all five stars, too.

So we were still losing.

Was there anything more we could do?

No, we were already doing everything.

The only reason I didn't give up was because of Bonnie. When she said, "We can do this," it gave me enough energy to keep going.

Have you met anyone on Hinge? I wrote to Chris on Thursday night. We'd been texting all week, but we hadn't really talked about anything deep. Just, How was your day? Fine. Yours? Good.

A few people, Chris wrote back.

I wanted details. Like who?

Like Heidi, Chris told me, who had a heart of gold and the cheekbones of a leopard, and Sam, a documentary film-maker who drove a teal scooter and ate orange-flavored Tic Tacs, which Chris thought was kind of gross, especially because it made her tongue all orange.

I didn't feel jealous, but I felt something that was probably a distant cousin of jealousy. Chris knew who she was.

Me, I felt lost.

I didn't give that away though. I acted like I felt as found as she did.

Yeah, I'm going out with Lex tomorrow night.

No longer nervous.

It took her four hours to respond with a lame thumbs-up emoji. I didn't want to admit that this annoyed me deeply, but it did.

CHAPTER 53

kit

Somehow I still had hope that the truth could remain buried forever. I'd been avoiding Chris's texts and calls. I just didn't want to deal with it. You might think this was selfish of me, and you might be right. People never expect the mother to be the selfish one, but, you know, all artists are ultimately very selfish.

On Friday evening, Bonnie and I were too stressed out to eat our pasta. All I wanted to be was her dog. If I were a dog, then nobody would expect anything from me, and I wouldn't have to go to this lunch at Chris's house.

"You're *coming*," Bonnie said.

"I already told you I'm coming. But I don't think we should tell Chris anything."

"Mom!"

"What!"

"Your friend Chris is being wrongly accused!"

"I'm just worried," I said. "What if Stevie never forgives me?"

"*You?* What if she never forgives *me?*"

CHAPTER 54

stevie

At fish restaurants, it's acceptable to hang pictures of people proudly holding up their caught dead fish. At steak restaurants, it is not acceptable to hang pictures of people proudly holding up a knife or a gun next to the cow they just slaughtered.

Why is this? Because fish have less blood? Because people fish for fun and for sport, but only farmers kill cows? Why is fishing a sport but cow-ing is not? Hunting is a sport, but not cow-ing.

Anyway, we're lying to ourselves. That's the point. We are a culture of liars.

7:30 pm. The Fishery in PB. See you there!

I reread Lex's text to make sure I was in the right place. I was. And she was six minutes late. I sipped my water and looked at the wall again. All the pictures were black-and-white, which gave them an old-timey feel, but the people in them wore modern clothes.

And then, a hand on my shoulder.

And a kiss on my cheek.

And, "Hey. Sorry I'm late. Traffic."

Lex sat across from me and smiled, creasing all the lines on her face. I wondered then if she liked to fish, maybe without a hat on. Maybe that explained why her face looked older than her age.

"No worries," I said.

"Have you been here before?"

"Never."

"It's the best," Lex said, and then she picked up the menu and started telling me what was good. The chowder, the crab cakes, the octopus salad. She took up all the room that was allotted to her on her side of the small table. She planted her feet far apart on the floor and leaned forward. Her body was saying, *I'm here now*. And also, *I got this*.

Her hair was bright blond and short except for one longer chunk in front that she kept swooping back with her hand. Her hands were small, because she was small—I would have guessed five feet three?—and they seemed industrious. They were hands that said, *I can build your furniture for you*.

"The sauce that comes with the calamari is killer," she said.

"Great," I said. We settled on that and some mahi-mahi tacos and when the waiter came, Lex ordered everything for us.

"And I'll take a Sapporo," she said.

"Water's fine, thanks," I said.

The menus were made of paper and limp as we handed them over.

"Are you sober?" Lex asked.

"I'm on a cleanse."

Lex said that was awesome, and then she told me about a cleanse she'd done once. The lemon-water-with-cayenne thing. She lost five pounds and then ate *like one Dorito* and gained it all back. So she probably wouldn't be doing another cleanse any time soon.

When the Sapporo came, she poured it into her glass at an angle, which is the correct way to pour beer. When she sipped, I felt like I had taken the sip for her. I could feel the lightness of bubbles in my mouth and the faint burn as they went down.

Lex took up space in the conversation in the same way she took up the literal space around her. "When was your last breakup? Do you date men, too? You're, like, zero percent butch. When did you come out? Ha. Don't you love that about gay first dates? It's always like, 'Hi, when did you come out?'"

I smiled. "When did *you* come out?"

"Not until college. I grew up in Texas."

"Do you date men, too?"

She threw her head back and howled at the ceiling. Then she brought her head back up and said, "Hell no."

And then she started telling me about her last breakup. Her ex's name was Shelly. Shelly was great for five years, super nurturing, a first-grade teacher, but they started to grow apart. And that was hard because Lex was the PE teacher at the same school. And they both still worked at this same school. "It's awkward. We kind of just avoid each other."

Lex kept talking. And talking. And talking. She'd apparently forgotten about the questions she'd asked me earlier, and I was glad because I didn't know how to answer any of them. When had I come out? Never. When was my last breakup? Never.

As Lex kept talking, I shifted from date mode to journalist mode. Who was this woman? And how was she still, forty-five minutes later, telling me about Shelly? Was this heartbreak on display or was it narcissism?

After the food, I excused myself to go to the bathroom. In the bathroom, there were more pictures of dead fish. I texted Chris.

I think this is a no.

————

How did I end up at that gas station again on the way home?

I don't know how fate works, not really, but it felt like fate.

This time, I knew right where the little chardonnays were kept: down on the floor right next to my shame. This time, I picked up a four-pack. And this time, when I went to the fridge to grab a bottle of water, Lauren Strong was grabbing a beer.

What did Lauren Strong look like when she turned and saw me?

She looked like shame.

Hummingbird fast, she took her hand off the beer bottle and closed the fridge door.

I tried to cover the four-pack with my blazer, but my blazer was so tight that it didn't really work.

"Hi!" Lauren said.

"Hey, Lauren."

Her eyes locked on the wine in my hand, so I took a different tack. I held it up higher and lied.

"It's for my sister."

Lauren Strong cocked her head. She remained silent for a long, hard beat. Then she reopened the fridge, took out the beer, and said, "This is for my sister, too." The worst part was how, right before she walked to the register, she tapped the air with her bottle and said, "Cheers."

Internally, I was frenzied. I was the water the waterfall pounds into, throbbing and roiling. But outwardly, I appeared calm. If you had seen me in that moment, you wouldn't have guessed that anything was wrong. I set the four-pack on the shelf that was closest to me, on top of a pack of powdered donuts, and moved swiftly out the door without looking back.

CHAPTER 55

bonnie

On Saturday morning, I knocked a mug off the counter by accident and it exploded all over the floor. Later, I would come to see this as the perfect bad beginning to a very bad day.

I cleaned up the pieces. It was five forty-five in the morning and still dark out. I hadn't slept well for days. When Stevie walked into the kitchen, I confessed immediately. "I broke one of your mugs."

"That's okay," she said, and poured herself some coffee. "How was Everett's last night?"

"I didn't go. I stayed here instead and got into a fight with Mom. It sucked."

"A fight about what?"

"Nothing. I'll tell you later. How was Brad's?"

"Good." Stevie flashed a smile.

"You seem less into him."

"No, I'm just . . . I don't know. I'm in a weird mood."

"Same."

"He's making us lunch today. Ceviche. What are you going to do?"

I was so sick of lying. "Mom and I have to run some errands."

"What errands?"

The problem was that a lie was never one lie. It was always the first of a painful series of lies. "Fabric store, whatever. Art errands."

Stevie sipped her coffee. She was holding the mug with both hands, and I don't know why, but she looked tiny to me for some reason, and like she needed to be comforted, so I hugged her.

She laughed. "Why are you hugging me right now?"

"I don't know," I said.

That was true. Because it was then that I realized maybe Stevie didn't need the hug. Maybe I did.

CHAPTER 56

chris

Bonnie had told me they were free for lunch. *Because Stevie will be at Brad's then. Don't tell her we're coming over, okay?*

I didn't feel good about this, but I agreed.

My first impressions of them as they stood outside my door were that Bonnie had grown up to be beautiful and Kit was glowing. "Are you using a new face cream or something?" I asked as they followed me to the table, where I'd already laid out lunch. I kept it pleasant for exactly two minutes, but that was all I could do.

"Please, sit."

We all sat. And then I just said it.

"I think you two are hiding something."

CHAPTER 57

bonnie

Other than this one lie, I was not a liar. I hated lying. Okay, fine, I'd cheated on Dwight a few times, so that wasn't very honest, but other than that, I swear there was nothing.

I heard someone say once that their goal was to be the same person to all people. Well, that was my goal, too. I don't think it's cool to be shady.

And this was how I felt about Stevie in high school. Everybody thought she was perfect, but when she got drunk, she turned into a different person. I can't tell you how many times I found her vomiting on herself. But then in the morning, her hair and makeup would be done and she'd look all perfect again. Mom and everyone else thought she was a star.

I'm sorry, but it just pissed me off. I didn't wear makeup. I was getting Bs. I wasn't that good or that bad, but at least I was honest. I didn't think it was fair how Stevie got away with so much. And she was such a bitch about it, too. That was the other thing. Her personality and how it shifted. At school, she kissed everybody's ass, but at home, she was mean. She made fun of my friends and my clothes and my hair. She said that she'd never want to be trapped on a desert island with me because the conversation wouldn't be that stimulating.

I never expected to do anything about this, though. I was just waiting for her to leave for college so I could be alone with Mom and our lives could be peaceful.

STEVIE FOR PRESIDENT.

I wanted to rip down her stupid posters. Every time I walked by one of them, I thought, *What a sham.*

I still remember the moment Brad approached me in the Taco Bell line at lunch. Those were the days of the chalupa, and I was obsessed with them. I didn't know Brad very well. He and Stevie had gone out a few times, but they weren't, like, an item. I had no idea how much he cared about her until he started talking.

Hey, I have a proposition for you.

brad

Here's what I remember: the shatter of a heart when it's broken for the first time.

I was in love with Stevie Green.

And then she dumped me.

And after that, I wasn't really thinking clearly. For the first time, I started to understand how love could drive a person to do something crazy, like murder.

I'd never cared about school politics, but I decided that running against Stevie would be my revenge. Taking away something she wanted seemed like a good way to hurt her. When I announced my candidacy, I thought she'd be pissed. I was so nervous when I went to school that day. I planned to keep my chest all puffed up and not back down. But Stevie didn't even acknowledge it. And she kept being nice to me, which really made me angry. When we passed each other in the hall, she smiled and waved like nothing big had happened, like she hadn't torn out my heart and then bulldozed it.

I realized that she was being so nice because she didn't

think I had a chance, and then I realized that that was probably right. I was popular, but Stevie was more popular. So I made a plan.

Before I did anything, I played out the worst-case scenario, which was that Bonnie would reject my idea and tell Stevie about it. I imagined how I would feel if that happened, and to be honest, I didn't think I could be knocked down any lower. I was already so depressed.

I waited a for day or two, thinking about my plan, and during that time, the plan got bigger. It went from Ruin Stevie to Ruin Stevie *and* Chris. I knew they had some weird thing together, and I knew they liked to drink on the sly. I had no idea they were doing coke, though, and even though I thought they might be secret girlfriends, I didn't fully believe it until I saw Bonnie's picture. All I had said to her was, "I need something incriminating, and I need you to do it, because they trust you. You can get closer than I can."

Bonnie knew immediately where she would go and when. "I'll go to Chris's house on Friday night," she said.

On Saturday, after I'd developed the film, I called Bonnie and said, "Money shot."

On Sunday, though, my brazen attitude turned to nerves. I thought I was going to get arrested at Kinko's. I photocopied the picture five hundred times, and as the pages came out, I kept looking at the *Cancel* button, wondering if I should press it. By the time I got to school at midnight to meet Bonnie, I was having some serious second thoughts.

"Are you sure we should do this?" I asked her.

"I'm positive," she said.

CHAPTER 59

kit

Bonnie confessed that very morning. She told me she was sick and needed to stay home. After Stevie left for school, I brought her some toast, and she said, "I did something bad, Mom."

I thought she was going to tell me she crashed the car.

After she admitted what she'd done, I wanted to blame Brad. "Did he talk you into this?"

"*I* took the picture."

The picture was now in my lap. I had no idea that Stevie was doing drugs. I didn't know about her relationship with Chris either, but after seeing them together, it made sense. Of course.

I knew that Stevie's drinking had gotten out of control, but she couldn't hear me when I told her that. "I'm getting straight As!" she would yell. This was true. She *was* getting straight As, and most of the time, she was a lovely person. Maybe I was overreacting.

I was naïve about the future that morning. I thought that

maybe the ordeal would have a positive impact. Stevie would see that she needed to clean her life up, and then she would become the perfect young woman I always knew she could be. What I didn't account for was the trauma, quite frankly. I grew up in a time when we didn't talk about trauma.

Bonnie, meanwhile, was panicking. "I have to tell her. But she's going to kill me."

I'm not saying this is right, but sometimes, as a mother, you just think to yourself: *I cannot fucking handle this.*

"We're not going to tell her," I said. "Ever."

CHAPTER 60

stevie

I didn't look at myself in the rearview mirror on my way to Brad's. I didn't ask myself who I was now, or what I was doing, or why. I was just barreling forward, inevitably and unstoppably, like a wave.

"Stevie, you're doing well. You're running a business, you're dating, you're getting more information, it's fine that Chris hasn't texted you back."

Yes, this was me talking to myself in the car.

———

Brad's perfect house, Brad's perfect body, the familiar allure of Brad's imperfect smile as he said, "Hey."

"Hi!"

Our kiss. My life as a rom-com.

I handed him the baguette I'd picked up on the way over.

"You didn't have to bring this."

"I know, but I wanted to."

Brad squeezed my waist with his big hand, and then we were in the kitchen, squeezing a few extra limes into the ceviche together.

"Yeah," Brad was saying, "it's sustainable swordfish."

What I thought: *I'm eating too much fish suddenly.*

What I said: "Sustainable, that's so great."

Daylight flooded Brad's living room, and the view of the ocean looked like a dream. I was chopping the cilantro very finely, and Brad was shaking blue corn chips into a speckled bowl, and then he said, "I'm going to go set the table." He gave me a quick kiss on the cheek and piled the napkins and the silverware onto two plates and walked out to the patio in that bouncy surfer way of his, and I thought about how, in an emergency, Brad would be a good person to have around. Fast reflexes. Strength. If San Diego caught fire right now, I would be glad to be here with Brad. Brad would save me.

When he came back inside, I was checking my phone.

"Anybody good?" he asked.

"Chris sucks at texting," I said.

"Chris," Brad said flatly.

"Yeah, Chris sucks-at-texting Dane."

I laughed.

Brad wasn't exactly glaring at me, but he was sort of glaring?

"Why are you looking at me like that?" I asked.

He rubbed his face like he was just waking up. "Nothing." He said "nothing" five more times—"Nothing, nothing, nothing, nothing, nothing"—as he moved around the kitchen island with the stealth of a tiger and kissed me with a passion that was surprising, and more surprising since it was only noon.

I kissed him back, trying to mirror his intensity because it was the easiest thing to do. I closed my eyes and thought, *Brad could be anyone. This mouth could be anyone's mouth.* But no, that was wrong. There were characteristics to Brad's kissing style that I recognized now. The switching of angles about every fifteen seconds, the blunt search of his tongue, the tentative nibbles of my lower lip.

On the way down to his bedroom, Brad stopped to say, "Look, no pool table," and I said, "So much potential," which would later seem like the one line that said everything. As he laid me down on his bed like a doll, the sense of impending doom that I'd been feeling all week was expanding. It felt like something nebulous that would have a sharp ending, like steam clouding the inside of a kettle, preparing to scream. Or it felt like someone was holding a lit match above a river of kerosene, saying, *Ready?*

Brad was lighting a candle now, and then he was lighting a second candle, and my heart was beating faster. I stayed completely still, watching him with a frozen smile, and when he looked at me, I could see that he had no idea how I was really feeling. He thought I was happy. He mirrored my smile, but his was real. I could see the future movie of our lives together playing in his head as he leaned in and kissed me, and then the kissing got faster, the tongue plunged deeper, he was making noises—"ah"—so I did, too—"ah"— and in the background was the sound of the ocean doing its thing, just being an ocean, just rocking tides back and forth until the end of time without worry or question, and Brad's usual smell of coconut and salt and pine disappeared under a pungent coat of sweat, and I was thinking about mammals and evolution and how maybe we'd lost the ability to appreciate each other's natural scents because of deodorant, and then I was wondering what I was going to say, because now his hand was up my shirt and this was only headed in one direction and I would have to say something soon, and then I was thinking of lies—*Don't feel good, maybe something I ate, forgot I have to leave in five minutes*—but none of them were very good, and then Brad was pulling my pants down and I was letting him and—

"Brad."

He lifted his head and smiled at me. "Yeah?"

Don't feel good, maybe something I ate, forgot I have to leave in five minutes.

"We have to stop."

At first he was sweet. He placed his hand gently on my cheek and said, "What's wrong?"

"I'm so sorry."

"Tell me what's wrong. What can I do?"

I moved his hand. I pulled my pants up. I scooted myself back and back and back until I was sitting with my back against the wall.

Brad sat up, too. "Stevie?" His voice was still sweet, and so was his face, and I couldn't look at him, so I looked at my hands, which looked like somebody else's hands, and I said, again, "I'm *so* sorry."

This was when his voice changed. There was no more sweet lilt. "Why are you sorry?"

"I can't do this."

Brad was shaking his head now. I knew what he was thinking. And then he said it, but with more cruelty than I expected. "Fuck you for getting my hopes up again."

"I'm so sorry."

"Yeah," Brad said. "Yeah."

I moved to the edge of the bed. I put on my shoes.

Brad stood and folded his arms across his chest. "I have to tell you something."

I waited.

"And I hope this hurts."

Brad, in that moment, wearing a graphic tee with a motorcycle on it, looked like a small, angry boy.

"You know that shit that went down in high school?"

"What about it?"

He flared his chest, but his arms were still crossed. "Bonnie and I did it. She took the picture, but it was my idea."

"Bonnie?"

"Why don't you want to be with me, Stevie?"

"I—"

"If it's because you're not into guys or something, you should just say that."

"I don't—"

"But you don't *seem* like you're not into guys. And I think you like me. I *know* you like me. But then you're checking your phone to see if Chris texted you! Like, who cares! We're having a nice time together! Who cares about Chris Dane!"

My heart was beating so fast. My body was on fire. Through the doorway, I could see the ocean, and I imagined it filling the house in one great sweep, and thrusting me out onto the edge of a waterfall, and then I imagined falling.

CHAPTER 61

chris

Brad's house was one of those La Jolla relics from the sixties or seventies that straddled the fine line between charm and disrepair. His driveway was big enough for two cars, but only his Jeep was there, with a surfboard on top, and propped against the fence were more surfboards, decorated with those bright red roses of his, and I had the same thought I'd had in high school, or maybe it was middle school, when Brad had invented his obvious motif. *Douchebag*.

Stevie's car wasn't on the street either. I called her, but it went straight to voicemail. *Hey! This is Stevie Green with Clean Green*—and then I was bounding up Brad's steps with an urgency that on the one hand seemed uncalled-for and on the other hand seemed like the only reasonable response.

I just had to tell her.

As a single set of footsteps approached the door from the other side, I thought about how good it would feel to punch Brad in the face, or in the stomach since he was a foot taller than I was. But then he opened the door, and it was suddenly a new story. The red splotches underneath his eyes, the moist rims of his nostrils, the vacant stare of a victim. Brad had just been destroyed, and then he had cried about it.

"Where's Stevie?"

"Why are you at my house right now?" he asked meanly.

We hadn't seen each other in a hundred years, but apparently we were picking up right where we'd left off: with Brad Rose despising me.

"I'm looking for Stevie. Is she here?"

"She left."

"Do you know where she went?"

"No."

"Okay, thanks," I said, and then I turned to leave, and Brad said, "Wait."

I stopped.

"Are you and Stevie back together?"

I almost laughed. "Brad, we were *never* together."

"Seriously?"

"Seriously."

And then the story changed again. I couldn't tell if Brad was ashamed or proud when he said, "I told her the truth about high school."

stevie

I'd planned to take my vodka somewhere nice, but I didn't even get out of the Ralphs parking lot. I just reparked the car in a new space at the very back, next to a dumpster, and started drinking straight from the bottle.

I want you to know that I didn't make the decision to do this.

It just happened.

The burn in my throat felt like an old friend, a shitty friend, and although I hated this old shitty friend, I loved her more than anything, too. Even before the buzz kicked in, I didn't care if anyone saw me. I had no shame. I had no guilt. I just wanted to feel better, and you know what? I did. I felt better instantly. Vodka was magic.

Obviously, I'd called Bonnie already. Somehow, I thought she might tell me it wasn't true and I would believe her. But no. She said, "I've been wanting to tell you so badly, but Mom—"

"*Mom* knew?"

That's when I heard Mom in the background. "Let me talk to her," she said.

I hung up, and then I turned my phone off.

So you can see why I bought the vodka. I knew right where it was, too, and which brand I would buy, because Ralphs was where I'd stopped earlier to pick up the baguette I'd brought to Brad's, and the vodka had been eyeing me then. In a way, or in all the ways, I'd just been waiting for a reason.

You might have expected me to be crying there in the car, or cussing my mother and sister out on the phone. You might have expected me to be screaming, "Oh my god, I'm totally not straight at all! Not even close! How could I have been in denial for so long?"

But no, it wasn't like that. When everything you thought you were building comes crashing down at once, there is no more building, and therefore no more pressure to build. There is also no more fear of falling. You've fallen, and now you're at the bottom, parked next to a dumpster, observing the rubble with distant calm. Everything is settled now, there is nowhere to be, the fight is over.

The answers weren't the ones I wanted, but the relief of having them was so great that I felt almost happy. The vodka helped. It wrapped me up in a blanket of *you're going to be okay. I know we hate each other*, it whispered, *but I love you more than anything, too.* Even as I got drunker, I felt clear. I knew this was goodbye vodka. I knew I couldn't go home. I knew that when the vodka was done, I'd call Chris. My apology would probably be slurred. I knew that, too.

Anyway, the last thing I remember is that it started raining.

CHAPTER 63

stevie

I thought I was in San Francisco at first. Foggy light. High ceilings. My head was full of cotton balls. My mouth was made of sandpaper.

I looked out the window, but it wasn't my window. And it wasn't San Francisco outside either. The window was very large and cut into many individual squares, and outside skinny palm trees swayed, their fronds thrashing madly in the rain.

The rain.

The dumpster.

The vodka.

The phone.

Brad.

Bonnie.

Mom.

Chris saying, "I'll come get you."

I propped myself up on an elbow, but too fast, and the movement sent a ringing shudder up my spine and into my head, and my head cracked into two pieces, and then into a thousand pieces, and I stopped breathing, so I told myself to breathe. I felt like I was dying, but I also knew the drill. Water, Advil, sleep it off.

I felt sorry for myself. I'd missed that about hangovers. And I'd missed, too, how a hangover reduced all of life's existential problems to the most basic set of needs. Water, Advil, sleep it off.

Water. In a pink-tinted glass on the bedside table and full to the brim. I ferried it toward my mouth carefully, hoping not to spill, and then I chugged it all, coughing weakly a few times at the end. Then I lay back, the glass still in my hand, and thought, *Chris buys pink-tinted water glasses?*

On the far side of the room was a white desk and a chair and an open door to a bathroom. To my left, a long dresser with three shelves, and a photograph of a bird on the wall, just its head. I didn't remember entering this room. What had Chris and I said to each other? I assumed I had apologized, and that it had been slurred, and that my car was still at Ralphs.

As I set the pretty pink glass back on the bedside table, I noticed two things. One, my phone was there. Two, I wasn't wearing my own shirt. It was a plain white V-neck that said *YEAH* on the front. I had to pull it away from me to read that. I lifted the covers to find a pair of light blue thermal underwear on my legs. Not mine either.

A light knock at the door.

"Yeah?" I said, then wondered if I'd said that because of the shirt.

"Hi," Chris said as she opened the door. I checked her

expression for signs of anger and found none. She didn't appear to feel sorry for me either. She just seemed, I don't know, like a stable human in some jeans and a gray blazer, possibly the same gray blazer she'd worn on the first day we ran into each other at the Pannikin.

"I got you a bagel." She picked up the water glass and set down a brown paper bag in its place. "Actually, I got you two bagels. One cinnamon raisin, one everything. I don't know what you like now."

"Oh my god, I love you."

Chris smiled. "I know you do."

And then we just stared at each other. It was a combination of *Who are you again?* and *How did this happen?* and *Of course this happened, it was really the only possible option.*

Or at least that's what I was thinking.

"I'm going to go get you some more water."

"And Advil, please."

"And Advil. And then I have to go back to work."

"What time is it?"

Chris checked her phone. "Twelve thirty," she said, and then she left the room, and I was left there with the smell of bagels wondering how it was twelve thirty in the afternoon.

Chris came back and put everything on the table—the water, the Advil, also a Gatorade and some saltines—and said, "This is a good hangover setup. You're lucky to have me right now."

"I know. Thank you."

She uncapped the Advil, handed me two pills, and I downed them with the Gatorade, the lemon-flavored one, and it tasted like heaven.

"I can't believe your mom knew," she said.

"I can't believe Bonnie . . . and Brad. What an *asshole*. I'm so sorry, Chris."

"I know. You told me a hundred times last night. We're good. You're forgiven." Chris shifted on her feet. "Listen, I have to tell you something."

"Oh god."

"It's very sad," she said. "But I think it might be a good thing, too."

"What?"

"Ursula de Santis died last night. Heart attack."

two months later

CHAPTER 64

stevie

Getting Clean with Stevie Green

Do you have a picture in your mind of the person you want to become? And a profound sense of how you'll *feel* when you become that person? Are you *almost* there, but not quite yet? If so, then let me help you!

The difference between a *clean life* and a *clean enough life* might look small from afar, but it's actually the Grand Canyon. Yes, you can put on a show for people. Yes, you can lie. Yes, you can live in a palace and wear great clothes and say the right things, but if your closets are packed to the brim with stuff you don't need, and if you also feel a little bit dead inside, then who cares how sparkly your life looks to other people? If it doesn't *feel* clean to *you*, then it's not.

Now you're probably like, *Well, okay, I think my life could be cleaner, and why isn't it already?*

Because you don't know what you want. And that's okay. Not knowing what you want makes you like everyone else.

It also really sucks, and you don't need to live that way any-more.

The solution is simple, but there are no shortcuts. Actu-ally, we're taking the long way to make sure we haven't left anything out. In order to figure out what you really want, we're going to start by getting rid of everything you *don't* want. You know that guess-and-check thing you used to do in math class? Have you heard that song "The Long Way Around"? It's like that. By saying goodbye to all the incor-rect answers, we'll land at the right one, and the right one is your clean and honest life.

It's time to free yourself.

It's time to become who you are.

———————

While Chris was at work, this is what I did. I wrote my book.

Yes, two months later, I was still at her house. At first, I didn't want to go home because Bonnie and Mom were trai-tors. Then I didn't want to go home because I wanted to be with Chris. Or, fine, I probably wanted to be with Chris the whole time. I'd probably imagined this ending when I'd called her from Ralphs.

More honestly, this was exactly the ending I had imag-ined.

But before I tell you about Chris, let me tell you about me. You, after all, are the top priority in your own life, are you not?

I hadn't decluttered a house in two months. What was the point now? I was number one. I have to tell you, the circumstances under which I became number one didn't allow me to feel like it was a real victory. Somebody had died, and that was tragic. I'd done nothing to earn my standing except remain alive. It wasn't exactly the heroic underdog win I had envisioned. But it was turning out that most of my visions of the future were incorrect, so it shouldn't have been that surprising.

I could have gone down a shame spiral about how it had taken me so long to come out. Thirty-seven! Ah! And I could have gone down a separate shame spiral about *why* it had taken me so long: because I was wasted for about twenty-five years and therefore not truly present while attempting to collect the necessary information.

And to be honest, sometimes I did start spiraling, but I tried not to spiral too far. What was the point?

When I forgot, I had Chris to remind me.

"Stop beating yourself up," she would say. "What's the point?"

It was amazing to be having conversations about all the things in my head not just with myself, but with a real live person who responded, and with kindness.

Maybe that's what a relationship is.

———

Chris started taking me to those meetings of hers. Well, she took me to a few, and then she told me to find some groups of my own so we could talk about each other behind each other's backs. I can't say too much about this, because it's like a secret society. Hopefully you understand. What I can tell you is that if you're trying to stop drinking, joining the secret society makes it a lot easier than doing it by yourself. You might think everyone in the secret society is crazy. They are. But mostly in a good way. Reformed-crazy is the best kind of crazy.

Two months into our relationship, Chris is still edgy about how little time I've been sober. "I'm *not* going to drink again," I tell her whenever she brings it up. And then we decide that there's nothing to be decided because this is a thing for time to decide.

The whole high school thing has become a joke around the house. I mean, sort of. If I eat the last apple, Chris says, "I *know* you did it!" I told her to stop being so passive-aggressive. She said she's trying. So the high school thing isn't hilarious yet, but it's as funny as it could possibly be at this stage.

I didn't want to forgive Bonnie and Mom, but I did. Even as I said, "I forgive you," I was thinking, *You two are assholes*. But then a strange thing happened. I started to believe my own forgiveness. Also, if I'm being honest, Mom called me "evolved" when I forgave her, and that stroked my ego. All I've ever wanted is for somebody to call me "evolved."

"I understand. I forgive you."

I just kept saying that, like a robot.

"Stevie, you have *evolved*."

"*Thank* you."

This conversation happened two weeks ago. Right afterward, I ate an entire bag of Pepperidge Farm Milanos, which did not feel very evolved, but whatever, I'm trying.

You know how when you go through a period of depression, you can't see how depressed you were until you're out of it? While you're depressed, you tell yourself, *I'm fine*, because you have to do that in order to get through the day, and it's only when you look back later that you realize how absolutely *not* fine you were.

I was not fine for a very long time, but I just couldn't see it, or I just didn't want to. I looked like a functioning person in the mirror, and therefore wasn't I a functioning person? The problem is that most pain is invisible, and lies are invisible, and the state of your heart cannot be measured by an app on your phone. What is the truth? What do you really want? How are you supposed to know? And when you think you do know, how can you be sure?

I've decided that the most important things in life are probably invisible.

I've decided, too, that the truth is always right in front of you, but that doesn't mean you'll ever see it.

Obviously, I've thought a lot about how decluttering factors into my trajectory. One analysis would be this: I decluttered myself from the outside in. I cleaned up my environment first, and the cleaner environment gave me the clarity to look at the deeper mess.

Another analysis would be about self-help gurus. Why

do they become self-help gurus? Because they need help. I think the advice that we find ourselves regularly giving to other people is probably the advice we most need to take.

So, the next time you want to tell someone what to do, maybe tell the mirror first?

What's my relationship to mirrors these days? you might be wondering.

Who am I?

Who am I now?

What about now?

Yes, of course I'm still asking these questions. And no, my scar hasn't gone away. Chris says it looks like an ice-skater performed an impressive move across my back. She also calls it "weirdly angelic." I smile every time she says that.

———

Bonnie and Everett are completely in love, as you might have expected, and now they're bickering about which type of dog to adopt. That's the short version. You can fill in the rest.

And Mom? Mom might be dating Bruce. She isn't committing to anything yet and she's focused on her dead dolls, which have really taken off, by the way. She's selling them on Instagram for five to ten thousand dollars apiece and she has eight thousand followers now. Don't ask me how this happened. Bonnie and I have about five thousand followers, and I've returned to my original feeling about Instagram, which is: I don't like it.

———

I'm going to end this story by telling you what happened yesterday.

Mom called and said, "Meet me at his cliff in twenty minutes before I change my mind."

"*His* cliff," I repeated.

"Bonnie's coming, too."

"Honey, we need to get in the car," I said to Chris, who was in the living room reading a book.

Can you believe I'm calling someone "honey"?

Me neither.

When we got to the cliff, Bonnie and Mom were already standing at the edge, next to the Monterey cypress tree that Mom had planted many years earlier. In Mom's hands: the red urn. Down Bonnie's cheeks: tears.

Chris and I hugged them without speaking. All around us, it was beautiful. The long line of the horizon, the easy light, the waves splashing over the seals resting on the rocks down below.

"It's time to say goodbye," Mom said. "Take off the top."

As I pulled the top from the urn, I could tell we were all feeling pretty poetic. There's a lot of expectation put on big life moments like these, and a heaviness, too, so I wasn't smiling. Honestly, I felt like I was about to eat a wafer at a Catholic church service or something. Serious. Ceremonial. That was the vibe.

Then Mom spilled a bunch of the ashes in the dirt by accident. Bonnie, who was crying so hard she could barely see, leaped forward to save them, but tripped and fell, and she was so close to the edge that Chris screamed, and then

Mom screamed, and then, once it was clear that nobody had died, Mom started laughing, and then we were all laughing.

Isn't it funny how long people wait to do things that take five seconds?

Mom dumped the rest of the ashes out of the urn, the ocean swallowed them up, and it was over.

But that's not the final image I want to leave you with.

The final image is this:

Chris put her hands on my face and kissed me, and after so many years of hating her guts, I realized that I loved her.

ACKNOWLEDGMENTS